PRISONER
IN TIME
A child of the Holocaust

PRISONER IN TIME

A child of the Holocaust

Pamela Melnikoff

The Jewish Publication Society
Philadelphia

2001 • 5761

The Jewish Publication Society
2100 Arch Street, 2nd floor
Philadelphia, PA 19103

Manufactured in the United States of America

01 02 03 04 05 06 07 08 09 10   10 9 8 7 6 5 4 3 2 1

Library of Congress Cataloging-in-Publication Data

Melnikoff, Pamela.
    Prisoner in time: a child of the Holocaust/Pamela
Melnikoff. −1st JPS ed.
        p.cm.
    Summary: In 1942, tired of hiding from the Nazis in a
Prague attic, a young Jewish man ventures out to an old
cemetery, from which he travels back to the sixteenth century
and witnesses another time of trouble for Czech Jews.
    ISBN 0-8276-0735-0
     1. Holocaust, Jewish (1939-1945)–Czech Republic–Juvenile
fiction. [1. Holocaust, Jewish (1939-1945)Czech Republic–
Fiction. 2. Jews–Czech Republic–Fiction. 3. Judah Loew ben
Bezalel, ca. 1525-1609–Fiction. 4. Golem–Fiction. 5. Time
travel–Fiction. 6. Czechoslovakia–Fiction.] I. Title.

    PZ7.M5163 Pr 2001
    [Fic]–dc21

                                                    2001029447

Thanks

I should like to thank Mr Ben Helfgott, who was himself a prisoner in Terezin when he was Jan's age, for his valuable help in answering my questions about the camp and checking my manuscript. I am also grateful to the late Dr Vivian Lipman for his advice.

I am particularly indebted to the books *Ghetto Terezin* by Z. Lederer, and *The Holocaust* by Bea Stadtler, for providing background details about Terezin.

Despite every effort, the publishers have been unable to trace a copyright holder for Pavel Friedman's poem, *I Never Saw Another Butterfly*. Any person wishing to claim copyright should write to Blackie and Son Ltd, who will be glad to rectify the omission of any formal acknowledgement for the use of this poem.

Preface

Although Jan and his family are fictitious characters, many of the people in this book really lived, and most of the events really happened.

Rabbi Judah Loewe ben Bezalel was a real person, although his creation of the Golem belongs to legend. His grave can be seen today in the Old Jewish Cemetery in Prague, near that of his friend Mordecai Markus Maisl, and his statue has been restored to the entrance of the New Town Hall. The Old-New Synagogue (the oldest synagogue in Europe) is still in use, and so is the Jewish Town Hall, but the synagogue built by Mordecai Maisl is now part of the State Jewish Museum.

Rabbi Dr Leo Baeck survived the war, and later settled in England, where he became Chairman of the Union for Progressive Judaism. He died in 1956, at the age of 83.

Adolf Eichmann, Commandant-in-Chief of the Terezin concentration camp, was put on trial for war crimes in Jerusalem in 1962. He was found guilty and hanged, and his ashes were scattered on the sea.

Pavel Friedman, Julie Ogularova, Helga Pollekova, Eva Winternitzova and Friedl Dicker-Brandejsova all died in the gas-chamber at Auschwitz in the autumn of 1944. The children's drawings and poems can now be seen on display in the State Jewish Museum, Prague. The butterfly in Pavel Friedman's poem has become the symbol of the doomed children of Terezin.

In all, some 15,000 Jewish children passed through Terezin. Fewer than 150 survived.

*This book is dedicated to the memory of Pavel Friedman,
Julie Ogularova, Helga Pollekova, Eva Winternitzova,
and all the other million-and-a-half Jewish children
who were murdered by the Nazis.*

1

The day that was to part Jan forever from his family began like any other. Dawn mist on the River Vltava rose to reveal the bridges, spires and glittering turrets of one of the most ancient and beautiful cities in Europe. The double procession of statues on the Charles Bridge marched majestically towards the opposite bank of the river, where Prague Castle and Saint Vitus's Cathedral lifted their proud pinnacles to the summer sky. It should have been a happy time and place for a twelve-year-old boy to be alive.

The sun peered through Jan's bedroom curtains. Jan stirred in his sleep, and then opened his eyes. Mother was calling him, telling him that breakfast was ready. Jan sat up in bed, and suddenly shivered. He remembered today was going to be different. When night came, the flat would be empty and the family gone. Jan's mother, grandfather, and two little sisters would have left Prague on board the transport train that was taking them and many other Jews to the mysterious place called Terezin, while *he* would be hiding from the Nazis in the attic of his friends the Nemecs.

Jan dressed quickly and went into the kitchen. The others were already seated at breakfast, Grandpa making the usual wry faces over his bitter artificial coffee, while Mother doled out lumpy porridge and Monika pounded Pavlina on the head with her spoon. Jan sat down at the table and gazed at them, trying to imprint their image firmly in his mind, so that he would not forget them. But he knew nothing could ever be the same again.

Nothing had really been quite the same for a long time. Their life had been changing, getting steadily worse, for the past three years. It had all really started on that bitter day in March 1939 when the German dictator, Adolf Hitler, had arrived in Prague behind his invading army.

He had come just before night, in a heavy snow-storm, riding in a car festooned with swastika flags. All day his tanks, motorcycle cavalcades and armoured cars had rolled into Prague, and now it was the Führer's turn. He looked straight ahead, smiling slightly, as the crowds that lined Wenceslas Square jeered, wept, shook angry fists, sang the Czech national anthem, and even dared to shout, 'Shame! Why don't you go home?' But he was not discouraged. Within an hour a curfew had been imposed; the people of Prague were huddled fearfully in their homes; German officers swaggered in the streets, and the swastika banner fluttered triumphantly above Hradzin Castle, where Hitler and his chief ministers were now having dinner.

Next day Father began to hear frightening rumours. Hundreds of Jews, it was said, were besieging banks, travel agencies and railway stations, desperately trying to get away from Czechoslovakia. Then came even worse stories: some Jews who were unable to leave had committed suicide.

'But why?' thought Jan. 'Why should Jews be more afraid than other people?'

He would soon understand why.

Jews had lived in Czechoslovakia in peace and contentment for many centuries. Most were of German and Austrian origin, and still had German surnames. They were prominent in business and the professions, and were well liked and respected by their neighbours.

Once the Jews of Prague had lived, for their own safety, in a walled ghetto near the river. But the walls and gates of the ghetto had been torn down long ago and the Jewish community had spread into the noble streets and squares of the main city. Jan lived with his family on the ground floor of a handsome stone house in Krizovnicka Street, just a short walk from the river and the ornate towers and statues of the Charles Bridge. His father, Dr Antonin Weiss, was a physician at a local hospital and also ran a private practice in their own home. His mother, Marta Weiss, was a pretty, elegantly-dressed woman who devoted much of her time to shopping, polite afternoon coffee parties and voluntary work among the poor. For the first six years of his life, Jan had been an only child; then Pavlina had been born, followed two years later by Monika. Mother doted on these two little late arrivals, decking them in hand-embroidered dresses and bright hair-ribbons. Jan privately thought them nuisances, though he tried not to tease them too much. The family was completed by Grandpa Max Freiberg, Mother's father, who had lived with them since Grandma died. He was an old man of soldierly bearing, proud of having served as an officer in the German army, and he sported a curling white moustache, smoked a pipe after dinner, wore his medals on special occasions, and told endless stories. The family had heard them often, but still listened politely.

To Jan it seemed a lovely life, though he had known no other. It was a life of delicious food, warmth, walks by the river, creamy pastries in the cafés, open-air summer concerts in the parks, sleigh-rides in winter, dinner-parties, visits to museums and fairy-tale castles and the theatre, holidays in spa resorts, and adults who were always kind to children.

It all came to an end that day in March 1939 when Adolf Hitler rode into Prague in the falling snow.

Jan knew that Hitler and his Nazi followers hated Jews and had heaped all kinds of hardships on the Jews of Germany and Austria. What he could not guess was just how quickly this example would be followed in Prague. Within days of Hitler's arrival, Jewish shop windows were being smashed; anti-Jewish posters and leaflets were being distributed; restaurants were putting up signs saying Jews were not wanted, and Grandpa was thrown out of the café where he had enjoyed his afternoon coffee and cake every day for the past thirty years.

That was only the beginning. Over the next three years, the plight of the Jews grew daily more miserable. Jewish shops and businesses were closed down and Jews deprived of their jobs. Father was dismissed from the hospital and forbidden to treat non-Jewish patients or employ non-Jewish women, which meant that Vera, his receptionist, and Ewa, Mother's housekeeper, both dear friends of the family, had to leave. Jews were put on strict food rations. There were no sweets for Pavlina and Monika; Grandpa sat sucking dolefully on his empty pipe, and Mother learned to make vegetable stews and pies.

But even this was not as bad as the isolation. It seemed to Jan that his world was closing in upon him. First he had to sit on a separate 'Jew bench' at school; then he was banished from school altogether. Jews were forbidden to leave their homes after dark, or to enter parks, cinemas and swimming-pools. When they travelled in trams they were crammed into the end carriages. Their radios were confiscated. Finally, the telephone was cut off, depriving Jan of his daily conversations with his best friend, Jaroslav Nemec. If Jaroslav had not been foolhardy enough to undertake the long walk from the other end of town, Jan would have felt abandoned. But he did come, at least two or three times a week, bringing school books and school gossip and -

best of all - fruit or a cake from his mother.

'People are so kind,' said Mother for the hundredth time, as she divided a large apple, the gift of Mrs Nemec, between Jan, Pavlina and Monika. 'That shopkeeper on the corner sold me some eggs today, and his wife asked after the family. They would be punished if the Germans found out. But have you noticed how good people are to us Jews, and how much they hate the Nazis? No, Jan, Father and Grandpa and I don't want any apple.'

'That's right ... apples make our teeth ache,' laughed Father. 'Yes, in some ways we're quite lucky. Other people are having a much harder time.'

Indeed, this was true. Prague was full of poor Jews with threadbare clothes and pleading eyes, who queued every day for free meals or food parcels at the soup kitchen set up by the Jewish community. Worse still were the rumours of atrocities being committed in other parts of Czechoslovakia. In towns like Bratislava, where Father's two brothers lived with their families, synagogues were being burned and Jews tortured and killed. 'If things don't get any worse for us,' said Father, 'then we must give thanks even for this.'

But things did get worse. In June 1940, the Nazis rounded up Jewish doctors and sent them to tend wounded German soldiers on the Eastern battlefields. Father was among them. As he hugged and kissed the family good-bye he whispered to Jan, 'You're the man of the house now. I rely on you to look after Mother and Grandpa and the girls.' Then he was gone, and loneliness and fear were suddenly added to the everyday miseries of boredom and an empty stomach.

Stomachs were growing emptier as the supply of ready money dwindled. All Jewish bank accounts in Prague had been stopped, and Mother was forced to sell her jewellery and household treasures to buy food. The only ornaments she refused to sell were the china coffee-pot and Venetian glass vase that had belonged to her

15

mother. On the day she sold a necklace to pay for a chocolate cake for Pavlina's birthday, two Nazi officers burst into the flat and, laughing, carried off the cake, the rest of the food, and what was left of Mother's jewellery. Jan silently willed them to leave Grandma's coffee-pot and vase alone and, miraculously, they did. Pavlina and Monika howled, and Mother cried with them, more upset by the loss of Pavlina's birthday cake than by her plundered jewels. It now occurred to Jan for the first time that they were in danger of starving to death.

There were other dangers, too. With the advent of the Jewish festival of Passover, the Nazis revived the ancient rumour that Jews killed Christian children to use their blood in the matzos, or unleavened bread. In the superstitious Middle Ages, Jews had been hanged for this 'crime', and now the Jews of Prague awaited riots and pogroms. But the people of Prague were wiser than their ancestors. They ignored the rumours, and three Passovers passed uneventfully.

'What we need is another Rabbi Loewe,' said Grandpa. The children often heard his tales of the legendary sixteenth-century Rabbi who had created a clay giant called the Golem and brought it to life as protector of the Jewish ghetto. But now the stories seemed more relevant.

'The priests spread the rumour of blood in the matzos, just as these accursed Nazis do now,' said Grandpa, 'and then some antisemite would put the body of a Christian child in a Jew's courtyard to incriminate him and all the Jews. But Rabbi Loewe knew exactly what to do. He made the Golem invisible, and the Golem walked through the streets and alleys of the ghetto, huge and silent, until he caught the villain red-handed. Then he tied him to the corpse, and delivered him up to justice. Nobody ever dared to try *that* trick again.'

'And then the Golem wasn't needed any more, and Rabbi Loewe got rid of him,' retorted Jan. 'Poor Golem

... I don't think that's fair.'

'Well, they say he became uncontrollable,' explained Grandpa. 'He ran through the streets tossing men and horses and even houses into the air.'

'I wish he would do that to the Germans,' said Pavlina. 'I wish he would throw those horrible soldiers who stole my birthday cake right over the rooftops.'

'Or spit on their heads,' added Monika helpfully.

In September 1941 came a new order. Jews above the age of fourteen were now required to wear a large yellow star of David, with the word 'Jude' inscribed on it. 'This should be a badge of honour,' sighed Grandpa, 'but I'm afraid the Germans have more mischievous things in mind.'

As winter drew on and the skies darkened, life became even harder. Unable to afford heating, the family shivered in their cold flat. Worse still, Jews were now being rounded up to clear the snow from the streets, and Grandpa was forced to join them. His eyes and nose were red and his moustache frozen when he came back indoors, and he promptly collapsed into a chair, shivering, coughing and wheezing.

'I'm not letting you do it again,' stormed Mother, as she brought him a bowl of hot soup and rubbed his icy hands and feet. 'I've always taken good care of you, and I'm not going to let you die of pneumonia now. I shall just tell them you're too old!'

'I have to take my turn, Marta,' said Grandpa patiently. 'All kinds of important people are down there, shovelling snow. I was sweeping the pavement just now with Professor Grünthal. We had quite a nice chat about whether Hamlet was mad or not.'

Mother burst into tears.

'I can't take any more,' she sobbed. 'I haven't heard from my husband for months, and I don't know whether he's alive or dead. We eat disgusting food and shiver with the cold. All my jewellery is gone and my shoes have no soles. And now *you* have to sweep the snow like a common labourer. Things can't get any worse! Please, God, don't let them get any worse!'

But even as she spoke, she knew that something much worse was about to happen. It was something everyone knew but no one dared talk about. Already Jews had been deported. Now it was rumoured that the trains that would carry the rest of the Jewish community away from Prague to an unknown destination were ready to leave. Some Jews, unable to stand the strain, killed themselves; others ran away and hid in the forests.

Most of them just sat and waited.

'Why can't I go with you?' asked Jan, yet again.

The summons to the Jews of Prague had come at last, and mass deportations had begun. Those whose names were on the list had received a printed card instructing them to assemble in four days' time at the railway station, where trains would be waiting to take them to Terezin, forty miles away.

'The Germans call it Theresienstadt,' said Grandpa. 'It's an old garrison town, named after the Empress Maria Theresa. I don't see how it can be so bad. After all, the Germans are civilized people. Some people even say they've turned it into a spa resort. Old Mrs Kovac paid a German officer a thousand crowns for a room facing south.'

'Why can't I go with you, if it's such a nice place?' urged Jan.

'Because the Nemecs have offered to hide you,' replied Mother, 'and I want to be sure that at least one of us is safe.'

'Why can't they hide us all?'

'Be sensible, Jan,' said Mother, stroking his hand. 'Their attic isn't big enough to take a whole family. Besides, they wouldn't have enough food for all of us. It's very good of them. They're risking their lives. Hiding a Jew is punishable by death. Now let me finish packing, there's a good boy.' She picked up Monika's battered teddy-bear and laid it tenderly in one of the suitcases.

'She's not taking that, is she?' cried Pavlina. 'It's only got one eye. If *she's* taking that ugly old thing, *I* want to take my doll's house.'

'Teddy's not ugly. He's my best friend,' retorted Monika.

'We can't pack your doll's house ... it's too big,' explained Mother patiently.

'It's not fair! *She* always does whatever she likes!' wailed Pavlina.

Once, Jan would have found his sisters' squabbling irritating, but now that he was about to lose them he suddenly realized how much he was going to miss them. Watching them eat their breakfast on this last morning at home, he wished he could have been nicer to all his family. But it was too late now.

'What are you going to tell the SS about Jan, Marta?' asked Grandpa. 'If they have our names on a list they'll want to know where he is.'

'I don't know,' replied Mother wearily. 'I'll say he's dead, or hiding in the forest. Don't worry, I'll think of something.'

'Are you taking food for the journey?'

'I thought I would make a few sandwiches. They might not give us a meal when we arrive, and the children will be hungry.' Mother looked down at the coarse grey bread she had been slicing, and her face crumpled. 'But how *can* I make sandwiches? I've nothing to put inside them.'

It had been arranged that Mr Nemec would call for Jan after breakfast and walk with him back to his house. It was the safest way; people seeing them together would assume Jan was Mr Nemec's son. When Mr Nemec arrived, tall and reassuring, his face grave and kind, he was carrying a small parcel, which he handed to Mother.

'My wife sent you some sandwiches for the journey,' he said. 'They're only cheese sandwiches, but she thought they might be welcome.'

Mother burst into tears, and Jan found himself wondering why - when she had so much that was important to cry about - she should cry over a piece of cheese.

The Nemec family lived in the upper half of a house on the other side of town between the National Museum and the Smetana Theatre. The small attic in the roof belonged to them, and it had been prepared very comfortably for Jan, with a flowered quilt on the bed, and matching curtains and cushions. There was a bookcase full of books, a table and chairs, a fringed lampshade, and even a vase of flowers. A narrow, winding staircase led to the family flat, enabling Jan to use the bathroom. Jan, still shattered by the last tearful parting from his family, felt warmed and soothed by the Nemecs' kindness.

'We do hope you'll be happy here for as long as you need to stay,' said Mrs Nemec, as she helped Jan unpack his bag. 'You should be quite safe here. All the neighbours are our friends and there's no one likely to betray us - unless the SS make an unexpected call, and they've never done that. I've made a special welcome dinner for tonight. I know you don't eat pork, so we're having grilled carp, and strawberries and cream, and a lovely chocolate cake.'

'I don't know how to thank you, Mrs Nemec,' Jan began, but Mrs Nemec interrupted before he could say any more.

'No thanks are needed, Jan. It's not just that you're our Jaroslav's friend ... Our family will never forget your father's kindness, especially when my poor mother was dying of cancer. How else can we repay our debt? Your father was a wonderful doctor, and all his patients loved him. I hope he's come to no harm, and that you'll all be together again soon. We're all praying for that day.'

Later that afternoon Jaroslav and his sister Jana came home from school and joyfully joined Jan in his attic, and soon afterwards Mr Nemec, who had vanished on some mysterious errand, reappeared. His face was grave, but he tried to sound cheerful when he spoke to Jan.

'I've just come from the railway station,' he said. 'I thought I would go down there to see your family off. Hundreds of people were there on the same errand. The station forecourt was quite crowded.'

For a few moments Jan was silent. Then, in a quavering voice, he asked, 'How were they?'

'They?'

'My mother, and Pavlina and Monika, and my Grandpa?'

'They seemed quite well. Calm and strong. I saw them getting into a ... into a carriage.'

'Were the SS in charge?'

'Yes.'

'W-were they kind to the Jews?'

'Yes. Reasonably kind.'

'Did the trains look comfortable?'

For some reason Mr Nemec seemed eager to change the subject. He turned abruptly to Jaroslav to ask about a test he had taken at school, and then the conversation turned to football. Jan had the uneasy feeling that there was something Mr Nemec would rather not tell him.

The rest of the evening passed pleasantly. Mrs Nemec brought Jan's supper up to the attic on a tray, and then the family joined him for an evening of dominoes and light-hearted conversation. It was ten o'clock before Mrs Nemec kissed Jan good-night, switched off the attic lamp, and ushered her family back down the winding staircase.

Jan lay alone in the dark, watching the moon through his attic skylight. In some unknown place the same moon was looking down on his family. Were they gazing at that bland silver face and thinking of him? What would become of them all?

His bed was warm and comfortable, and his stomach full of the best food he had tasted in three years. Where were his family sleeping that night, and were they hungry? He remembered the morning's parting, with his mother urging him to be strong and survive for all their sakes, and tears filled his eyes.

At last he fell asleep, and dreamed that he, Mother and Father, Grandpa, Pavlina and Monika were reunited round the family table in Krizovnicka Street.

It was as well that Jan did not know, at that moment, that he and his family would never sit together round a table again.

2

A year passed very slowly.

Jan's only view of the passing seasons came through his attic skylight. The brilliant blue sky of summer gave way to a golden autumnal glow, and then came lowering black clouds, and snowflakes piled up against the glass. Jaroslav and Jana came home from school in fur hats and heavy boots, red-cheeked and blowing on their frozen fingers, and there was hot soup and stodgy pudding for dinner every night. Then the snow melted from the skylight, and spring was on its way again.

All this time Jan had scarcely been out of the attic, and never out of the house. It was unbearable, especially when the sun was shining, and he longed to be out of doors. While *he* had grown taller, the attic seemed to have shrunk. The best time of day was when the young Nemecs arrived home from school, Jaroslav bringing him text-books and homework assignments as well as news of the other boys, while Jana, who was two years older, passed gossip about her friends, their clothes, make-up and boyfriends, and their quarrels with their parents. Jan would normally have scorned such girl-talk, but now he pounced eagerly on every shred of conversation.

Sometimes Mr or Mrs Nemec brought him more important but less pleasant news, gleaned from the foreign radio broadcasts to which they listened on pain of death. After four years, Europe was still at war.

Across the Channel, Britain stood firm, but Czechoslovakia and most other European countries remained under Hitler's heel. The news nearer home was even less cheering. Practically all the Jews of Prague had now been transported - some to Poland, but most of them to Terezin. German families had been moved into their homes.

'But I'm sure it will soon be over and your family back home again,' said either Mr or Mrs Nemec with forced heartiness after delivering each news bulletin. 'Hitler *can't* hold out for very much longer. Sooner or later the occupied nations will *have* to rise up and overthrow him.'

For Jan the worst day of all that year in the Nemecs' attic was the day of his barmitzvah. On his thirteenth birthday a Jewish boy officially becomes a man, and all his family rejoice. If Hitler had never come to Prague, thought Jan, he would even now be standing, draped in a new silk prayer-shawl, in the pulpit of his family's synagogue, called upon for the first time in his life to read from the scrolls of the Law. Father and Grandpa, both in new suits, would have been standing beside him, beaming with pride, while Mother, Pavlina and Monika, all in new hats, would have smiled down at him from the women's gallery. And afterwards there would have been a splendid party, and speeches, and presents ... Though Jan tried to tell the Nemecs how important the day should have been, they did not really understand. Mrs Nemec baked him a cake with thirteen candles, and they all sang 'Happy Birthday', but it was not the same.

One day Jan looked up at his skylight and realized that another spring had arrived. Outside, the world must be beautiful, he thought, with the sun shining and all the trees in bloom. His legs desperately needed stretching, and he felt as if he were suffocating. 'Surely,' he thought, 'it wouldn't do any harm if I were to go out for a little while? Just for a very short walk? After all, the

Gestapo have never called here yet. Why should they come today? I shall die if I can't get some fresh air.'

The Nemec flat was empty. Mr Nemec was at work, the children at school, and Mrs Nemec had gone shopping. If he slipped out just for an hour, he thought, nobody need know.

Jan put on a warm jersey and crept down the spiral staircase, his heart thumping with fear and excitement. 'That's the easy part over,' he said to himself. 'Now for the harder bit.'

He need not have worried. The next stretch of staircase was empty, and the door of the downstairs flat was closed. There was nobody to see him. Jan crossed the entrance hall, and stood hesitating for a moment before opening the front door. A rush of warm, velvety air greeted him, and an indefinable perfume. He went towards them gladly, and the heavy door closed after him.

To Jan, Prague seemed, at that moment, the most magical city that had ever existed. In the April sunlight it was a city encrusted with gold, its squares, churches and palaces laid out like the gems in a jewel-box.

He passed the imposing facade of the State Museum, and emerged into Wenceslas Square, a long rectangular boulevard lined with shops, restaurants and hotels and overlooked by the statue of King Wenceslas on his prancing steed. It was here that Hitler had ridden in triumph and the Czech people had stood jeering, but now there were only a few jackbooted Nazi officers to be seen, smiling as they kept a wary eye on the crowds strolling along the pavements. Jan joined the throng, looking happily into shop windows and trying to ignore the swastika banners and the portraits of Hitler. Then, leaving Wenceslas Square, he followed the narrow, winding streets to the Old Town Square, one of the loveliest places in Prague, with its ancient houses intricately carved, painted and gilded. Here too stood the many-steepled Tyn Church and the Old Town Hall with its marvellous astronomical clock, where little mechanical figures par⁻ded on the hour. From here it was only a short walk to Dr Vacek Square, with its modern town hall where the statue of Rabbi Loewe, creator of the Golem, had once stood. When he was younger, Jan had been fascinated by the imposing stone figure with its stern features, tall hat and flowing beard and robes. He had gazed up into the brooding face and wondered what kind of person the Rabbi had been. But now the statue was gone. Early in the war it had been removed by the Czech people and hidden, so that the Nazis could not destroy it.

Only a very short distance separated Jan from Krizovnicka Street and his old home, but he avoided it. Seeing the house where he had been brought up would have been too painful. Besides, he had been away too long from his attic; Mrs Nemec might be back from her shopping, and then he would be in trouble. Jan regretfully turned back and retraced his steps to the Nemecs' house, dreading the moment when he would have to go out of the sweet, warm, perfumed air into his cramped and musty hiding-place.

Mrs Nemec had already returned home, and Jan stiffened, expecting a scolding. But he was not prepared for what actually happened. Her face was no longer kind and placid but pale and distraught; her hair was dishevelled, and she turned on Jan angrily.

'How could you do this to us?' she cried before he could speak. 'Jan, how could you be so stupid? We've been betrayed! My children ... my poor children are in danger because of you.'

'But what's happened?' asked Jan, feeling his heart lurch. 'I only went out for a little while.'

'It was long enough for someone to see you. A Nazi-lover, a member of those accursed Hlinka Guards, recognised you. He was passing as you came out of the house, and he knows you're Jaroslav's friend. He reported us at once to the Gestapo, and they called here. Luckily there was no one at home. The people downstairs spoke to them ... *they* warned me.' Mrs Nemec broke off and grabbed Jan's sleeve urgently. 'For God's sake, Jan, you must leave at once! They'll be coming back ... they could come at any time ... and if they find you here we'll all be lost. It's a capital crime to hide Jews.'

'But where shall I go?'

'Anywhere, as long as it's far from here. And be sure to stay away for a few days. I must go up to the attic and hide all your things.' She turned to the bewildered Jan and gave him a little push. 'Hurry, what are you waiting for?'

So now he was back in the streets of Prague, but this time it was a different city. Its magic had gone. It seemed to him that all the SS men were watching him; that the people in the streets were turning to stare at him; that the eyes in the Hitler portraits followed him. And he had nowhere to go.

This time he made for the Jewish quarter, Josefov, just north of his old home in Krizovnicka Street. Here the walled Jewish ghetto had once stood, but the maze of cobbled alleys had been replaced by wide streets and fine stone houses. All that was left of the ghetto was its six splendid synagogues, its medieval cemetery and ceremonial hall, and the Jewish Town Hall with its pink-washed walls, green clock-tower, and unique Hebrew clock whose hands went backwards like the language itself. The synagogues were closed and abandoned now, but Jan knew them all. There was the High Synagogue, with its massive chandelier and the gold stars on its pale walls and vaulted roof; the Klaus Synagogue, with its magnificent painted ceiling, blue and green stained-glass windows and pink marble women's gallery; the majestic Pinkus Synagogue; the Maisl Synagogue, which had twenty columns supporting its roof, and the Spanish Synagogue, in Moorish style like the Spanish Alhambra. Older and more mysterious than any of these was the Old-New Synagogue, built in the thirteenth century in the style of a Gothic church. Inside it was dark, dank and austere, with black wrought-iron chandeliers, and Hebrew inscriptions painted in black on the stark whitewashed walls. The tapestries that concealed the Ark were old and faded, and so was the banner hanging from the vaulted roof that had been presented to the Jewish community in 1648 by the Emperor. In the pulpit of this synagogue Rabbi Loewe had once preached; here stood the throne-like wooden chair where he had sat at prayer, and somewhere in the roof lurked the dark attic where, according to legend, he had created the Golem from the mud of the River Vltava.

But none of these buildings held any refuge for Jan. They were places where the Gestapo might easily search for fugitive Jews. He turned off the road into the cemetery, which lay quietly in the shadow of blossoming trees. There would be no one there, other than the dead, and *they* would not harm him.

This graveyard, which dated from the early fifteenth century, was one of the strangest places in Prague. It contained some twelve thousand gravestones, for throughout the centuries coffins had been buried in layers, one above the other, and the ancient stones, slanted and battered with age, crowded in upon each other as if some giant hand had scattered them. Jan had enjoyed walking here with his parents as they pointed out the inscriptions and carvings on the stones. Many famous medieval scholars, historians, astronomers and mathematicians lay under them, and the sculptures represented their names or professions. Some of the carvings were of doctors' instruments or tailors' scis-

28

sors; wives and mothers were represented by candle-sticks, and priests by hands raised in blessing. Grandest of all was the tomb of the rich and powerful Mordecai Markus Maisl, once Mayor of the ghetto and financial adviser to the Emperor, who had built the Maisl Syna-gogue and the Jewish Town Hall and had also estab-lished the cemetery. Jan did not stop to look at any of them. He went directly to the tomb of Rabbi Loewe.

This was an imposing stone sarcophagus carved with lions, for the name 'Loewe' meant lion. Wedged among the stones were numerous small pieces of paper, messages and petitions from the pilgrims who had come seeking the Rabbi's help. There was a slot in the tomb in which - so Jan had heard - Jews on the eve of transpor-tation to Terezin had desperately placed their treasures for safe-keeping.

On impulse, Jan slid his hand into the slot, and his fingers closed over something very small and hard. When he pulled out his hand he saw he was gripping a tiny golden bird with outstretched wings and ruby eyes.

'I wonder who owned this,' he thought. 'Perhaps they're dead now, and this bird will stay here for ever.' He gently rubbed the bird with his finger-tip, and as he did so he found himself speaking aloud.

'Rabbi, I know there were troubles for the Jews in your time,' he said, 'but they weren't as bad as ours. Nothing could ever be as bad as ours. I wish I could go back to your time ... '

Here Jan broke off. A sudden dizziness came on him, and the graveyard seemed to swim, then dissolve into darkness. He closed his eyes and waited for the dizzi-ness to subside. It did after a few moments, and Jan warily opened his eyes again. Then he wondered if he had fallen asleep and was dreaming.

The graveyard looked quite different. Most of the stones had vanished, and those that remained stood erect, their inscriptions neat and newly carved.

'What's happened?' he asked. Then he turned to look again at Rabbi Loewe's tomb, and gasped in disbelief. *The tomb had disappeared.*

3

Still clutching the golden bird, Jan left the cemetery and turned towards the street that led to the Old-New Synagogue. He had noticed that he was now wearing different clothes - a tunic and breeches that seemed to belong to a past age - and he wanted to see what else was different.

'I don't believe this!' he thought. 'Such things don't happen.' Suddenly he stopped and stared.

The wide street he had expected to see had vanished, and in its place was a narrow, cobbled alley with a ditch down the middle, overflowing with rubbish and rancid water. On either side, narrow, gaunt and so tall that they almost shut out the sky, were timber-framed houses like the ones in some medieval picture-book. Off this street ran similar ones, twisting and winding to form a maze of narrow, sunless alleys and Jan saw, as he explored them, that the area was surrounded by a high stone wall. At the end of one alley he glimpsed an archway surmounting a pair of massive gates, guarded by a thickset man carrying a halberd.

'It's a walled city,' thought Jan. 'I'm back in Rabbi Loewe's ghetto. I wished to be back there ... and now I am. But how did it happen?' And then he remembered that he had been stroking the golden bird. Could it be some kind of magical amulet? Jan opened his hand and looked at the bird fearfully.

There was a smell in the air that reminded Jan vaguely of dustbins and the latrines he had helped clean when he was at summer camp. He wrinkled his nose, and wondered in which of these stinking alleys he would find the Old-New Synagogue now. He need not have worried. He soon recognized the building, which had changed little, and he went towards it eagerly, knowing who might be waiting for him.

Jan went down the steps and through the low arched doorway that led into the synagogue. A hum of voices greeted him, and the sound of chanting, and he realized that the evening service was in progress. He had been surprised not to find people in the streets, and now he understood why.

Inside, the synagogue looked the same as he had always known it, yet different. The tapestry covering the Ark had suddenly grown bright and new, and no imperial banner hung from the vaulted roof. But it was the congregation that looked strangest of all in Jan's eyes. Some of the men who stood swaying in prayer wore long, sleeveless caftans over under-tunics; others, far grander, were dressed in embroidered doublets and velvet cloaks. But whether their clothes were simple or grand, they all wore blue, pleated ruffs, and all - Jan noticed with a shock of recognition - had a yellow badge, in the form of a circle, stitched to the left breast.

Jan sat down on the end of a wooden bench, relieved that the other people scarcely glanced at him. After a few moments a majestic figure mounted into the pulpit, and Jan's heart beat faster. The image created by the sculptor of the statue outside the New Town Hall was not far from the truth. The imposing height was there, and so were the flowing robe and long beard, but the features of the real Rabbi Loewe were less stern than those of the statue, and the eyes under the bushy brows looked kind.

Encouraged, Jan leaned forward and listened. The Rabbi was preaching a sermon on the virtues of charity, and Jan was surprised to find that he spoke German, not Czech. Then his thoughts began to stray from the sermon as he wondered what to do when the service ended.

The final hymn was sung at last, and the congregants began to stream out of the synagogue, making obeisance to Rabbi Loewe as they departed. Their wives, who had been praying in an ante-chamber, now joined them, and Jan saw that they wore quaint linen caps with pointed wings on either side, some trimmed with blue stripes and others with yellow.

When everyone else had gone, and the Rabbi was about to leave, Jan approached him. Rabbi Loewe looked up enquiringly, and Jan's nerve almost failed.

'Your pardon, Rabbi,' he began, surprised to find that he too was speaking fluent German. 'I am an orphan newly arrived in Prague. I ... there was a pogrom in ... in Brno, and I was the only survivor.' Here he dug his knuckles into his eyes, and the Rabbi sighed.

'Every day I hear of some fresh sorrow,' he said. 'I didn't know about the pogrom in Brno. When did it happen, child?'

'Yester ... I mean, last week. I walked most of the way here, and a farmer gave me a lift on his cart.'

'Do you have other family?'

Jan shook his head.

'What is your name?'

'Jan Weiss.'

'Jan?' The Rabbi wrinkled his brow. 'What kind of name is that for a Jewish boy? Now "Weiss" is a sensible name - but Jan? I shall call you Yankel. That's a good Jewish name,' he said, and although his voice was stern his eyes twinkled. 'Now, tell me, Yankel, how can I help you?'

Jan already had his answer prepared.

'Please let me be your servant, Rabbi,' he said

33

eagerly. 'If you take me into your household I promise to serve you faithfully. I need a roof over my head, and friends.'

'Do you have no friends nearer home?'

'But I want to be with you!' cried Jan desperately. 'I came here especially to find you.'

The Rabbi looked surprised.

'Has my fame spread as far as Brno?' he asked. 'There are many renowned Rabbis in Bohemia, so why should you seek me out?'

'Because you are the greatest of them all,' cried Jan, too excited now to know what he was saying. 'Who has not heard of Rabbi Judah Loewe ... teacher, scholar, and creator of the Golem?' Then he stopped, suddenly frightened, because the Rabbi was staring at him open-mouthed.

'Who are you?' he asked at last, and Jan saw that all the blood had drained from his face and that his hands were shaking. 'Where do you come from? How can you read what is in my mind?'

'What do you mean, Rabbi?' asked Jan, puzzled.

There was a silence, and then Rabbi Loewe said, 'How did you know about the Golem? No one knows it but myself. *I was going to make him tonight.*'

4

For a while Jan and the Rabbi faced each other in silence, while Jan frantically wondered what explanation he could possibly offer. The truth was plainly unthinkable ... no one would believe it. Then it suddenly occurred to him that Rabbi Loewe was the one man, above all others, who *might* accept such a tale. He had studied the Cabbalah, the book of Jewish mysticism; he had written books on the supernatural; he was believed by his disciples to be a miracle-worker; moreover, was he not preparing that very night to create a living man in the dark attic above his synagogue?

So Jan told the Rabbi his story, hesitant at first, and then growing bolder as he saw the frown fade from the Rabbi's face.

'How can *I* disbelieve you?' he said at last, echoing Jan's thoughts. 'My followers say that *I* can travel in time. They even insist that I can turn base metals into gold and cause castles to fly. And also there is the Golem. ... For myself, I have always believed that nothing is impossible. So, now, Yankel, will you show me the golden bird that brought you here?'

Jan took the bird from the pocket of his tunic and gave it to the Rabbi, who looked at it intently.

'I have never seen an amulet like it before,' he said, 'but it must have a powerful magic. Take care of it, Yankel. Your life may depend on it.' He handed it back to Jan, and then added, 'So you wish to join my household? As my servant? How can I refuse such a plea? Besides, I know now that I need someone to help me create the Golem. It is scarcely a task that I can undertake alone.'

Jan felt as if he were dreaming. All his life he had listened to Grandpa's tales of the Golem. Now, by some incredible magic, was he himself to become a character in that ancient legend?

As they left the synagogue, the Rabbi said, 'It might be as well if my family and servants did not know the truth about you. We shall say you were orphaned in a pogrom in Brno, and I shall rely on you to invent and accept our time as well as you can.'

At these words, Jan stopped and gazed at the Rabbi in dismay.

'Can I ask you something, Rabbi?' he said hesitantly. 'Something I need to know?'

'Whatever you wish.'

'What is the date?'

'The first of Nisan. In less than two weeks it will be Passover ...'

'No, I don't mean that. I mean the year.'

'This is 1589,' replied the Rabbi, and his lips twitched with amusement. 'I agree, Yankel. It *is* sometimes useful to know which century one is in.'

The Rabbi's wife and daughter and his servants greeted Jan without any apparent surprise. They knew all about pogroms and orphans, and they were quite used to seeing such sad creatures brought into the sanctuary of their house.

The household was also used to entertaining more illustrious people, to Jan's surprise. He had thought a ghetto would be a poor and persecuted place, but now, seated at the Rabbi's table, he learned that it could also be a place of wealth and distinction. The Rabbi insisted that Jan should be treated as a member of the family instead of being banished to the kitchen with the servants. Now, as he steadily munched his way through a lavish supper of broth, baked trout, roast goose, sugared fruits and marzipan, he heard surprising references made to the foreign ambassador who had dined with the Loewes the previous week; to the distinguished astronomer who was to dine with them in the week to come, and to the courtiers, rich merchants and scholars with whom the Rabbi was apparently on friendly terms. Equally astonishing was the sumptuous appearance of the Rabbi's house. Jan had imagined that the gaunt and rickety exteriors of the ghetto houses must conceal equally gaunt and rickety interiors, but the parlour in which the family was eating, though cramped, had oak panelling and carved and polished furniture, rich hangings, velvet tapestries and candles in heavy silver candlesticks.

But what surprised Jan most of all was the familiar way in which the Rabbi's wife - the Rebbetzin, as she was called - and their daughter Varealina behaved towards the esteemed head of their household. Jan had always thought of Rabbi Loewe as an almost mythical being, a great teacher and scholar, a majestic statue and a crumbling tomb. It had never occurred to him that this miracle-worker could also be a man, a husband and father just like any other, and he listened entranced as the Rebbetzin urged the Rabbi to eat second helpings of everything, and the Rabbi for his part teased his daughter about the lavish new dress she had just had made for the forthcoming Passover festivities.

'But, Father,' said Varealina, a pretty girl of about eighteen, 'you wouldn't want your daughter to look like a pauper, would you?'

'A pauper is one thing, and a royal princess is another,' replied the Rabbi, trying to sound disapproving. 'You should set a good example to my flock. How can I preach modesty and decorum from my pulpit when my own daughter decks herself in gold embroidery fit for an emperor? There are laws that forbid Jews to wear expensive clothes and ornaments - not that anyone in my community seems to have heard of them.'

'You wouldn't want Mistress Maisl to outshine us, would you, husband?' asked the Rebbetzin with a demure smile.

'Indeed, I would. Mistress Maisl is the wife of the richest man in Prague. *He* builds synagogues and lends money to the Emperor, whereas I am only a humble Rabbi.'

Jan, listening to them, marvelled. He had always known Mordecai Maisl as the occupant of the most magnificent tomb in the Jewish cemetery. Now it seemed that he was alive and living nearby, while his wife flaunted herself in the kind of splendid clothes that Jews were not supposed to wear.

To Jan's relief, neither the Rebbetzin nor Varealina asked *him* many questions about his past life. Perhaps they did not want to cause him pain; perhaps they were too busy gossiping; whatever the reason, they contented themselves with enquiring sympathetically but briefly about his family. Jan replied, equally briefly, that they were all dead, crossing his fingers under the table as he did so. By not talking, he told himself, he could avoid giving himself away.

Even so, it was difficult. Life in the sixteenth century seemed to be different in so many ways, all of them unpleasant. Jan, used to the instant light and heat of gas and electricity, found it hard to accept a darkness only partially dispelled by firelight and candlelight. Even the blazing log fire in the hearth roasted half of him while leaving the other half to freeze, and he longed for the great tiled stoves that heated the rooms at home. And then there were the rooms themselves; compared with the spacious, high-ceilinged rooms of his own time, those in the Rabbi's house were small and poky, the ceilings low, the windows narrow behind their heavy shutters, the stairs steep and winding, and an odour of chill and damp everywhere. Peering into the kitchen he had noticed that a great effort was being made to cook the food, which was turning on spits or bubbling in huge cauldrons, supervised by a sweating, red-faced cook, and when it finally arrived it tasted strange to him. There was no hot water, except that which was drawn from the well and heated over a fire, and, asking for the lavatory, he was disconcerted to be directed to a stinking earth latrine inside one of the walls. When he was finally shown to a small bedchamber, lit by a single candle in a pewter candlestick, he found that the bed, though well-provided with goose-feather pillows and quilt, was not nearly as comfortable as his own bed at home - or even his bed in the Nemecs' attic.

Not that it mattered. He would not have to stay in bed long. When all the household was asleep, the Rabbi would rouse him and take him to the dark place above the Old-New Synagogue where the Golem was to be born.

Jan lay holding his breath, willing himself to stay awake, and waiting for the Rabbi's knock on his door.

Jan was nearly asleep when it came. He got up, quickly pulled on his clothes, and followed the Rabbi's dimly flickering lantern down the steep staircase and into the street. All was silent, for a curfew prevented Jews from leaving the ghetto at night or receiving visitors from outside, and most people went to bed early. Windows and doors were shuttered and bolted and, although a full moon was shining, the dark houses, tall and gaunt, shut out the brilliance of the sky. Nevertheless it was still possible to recognize, among the steeply pointed rooftops, the distinctive triangular upper storey of the Old-New Synagogue.

Jan shivered in the cold night air, though his heart

was racing with excitement. The Rabbi must also be feeling cold, he thought, for the hand that held the lantern was shaking. Then, to his astonishment, Jan realized that his guide, so stern and strong, was trembling not with cold, or excitement, but with fear.

'God be with us, Yankel,' said the Rabbi at last, gripping Jan's shoulder with tremulous fingers as they stopped at the small door that led to the synagogue's attic. 'Are we committing a sin? Surely it is a fearful thing to make a man! Should we not leave matters of life and death to God?'

'God works through man, Rabbi,' replied Jan eagerly. 'My father used to say that. He was a doctor, and he said it was God who healed people through his hands.'

'Ah, he spoke well, Yankel,' replied the Rabbi. 'It will be God, working through *my* hands, who shapes the Golem; no mere man has the power to create life. But I can wait no longer ... As Easter approaches,and Passover, my people begin to huddle in their houses, waiting for some Christian corpse to be hidden in a Jewish courtyard and the old blood-ritual accusations and pogroms to start all over again. As Jews, we put our trust in God, but we also need a human - or perhaps I should say superhuman - protector.'

'I know, Rabbi,' said Jan eagerly. 'My grandfather told me.'

'Ah, I forgot, Yankel. *You* already know the end of the story. How could I forget that? Tell me, child, did good come of it? Was I punished?'

'Yes, good did come of it. And you were praised for it, not punished.'

Thus reassured, the Rabbi lifted a heavy key from the bunch at his belt, unlocked the door, and opened it. Ahead soared another steep staircase, its upper regions lost in darkness. Following the rabbi's wavering lantern, Jan marvelled yet again at the strong legs of the people of the sixteenth century.

At the top of the stairs lay the famous attic, flooded by the moonlight that poured through its narrow windows. It was a large room, musty-smelling, its roof high and pointed, its floor thick with dust. All around lay piles of old prayer-books and heaps of worn and tattered prayer-shawls. But Jan's eyes were at once drawn to several large bulging sacks propped in a corner of the attic. Alongside, spread on some sackcloth on the floor, was the largest suit of clothes Jan had ever seen. There were a tunic, breeches, a coat, hat and boots, all big enough to fit a giant. Jan's heart leaped, for he knew who was going to wear them.

Rabbi Loewe set down his lantern, and began to pray. His prayers seemed interminable, and Jan shifted his feet impatiently. But the Rabbi finished at last, and opened the first of the sacks. Jan, watching eagerly, saw a great mass of thick mud ooze out onto the floor. The other sacks were emptied onto the pile till it was higher than Jan.

'Freshly gathered at dawn from the bed of the Vltava - one sack at a time,' explained the Rabbi. 'God guided my hands then; may He continue to guide them now.' And so saying, he placed his long, delicate fingers on the sticky pile and began to work the mud. It was, thought Jan in awe, as if he were making mud-pies or a sand-castle. At first the shape that was growing under his fingers remained unrecognizable, but eventually Jan began to make out the limbs and features of a gigantic man.

'Will the Golem be able to speak?' he asked. 'Will he be able to think?'

'That is as God wills it. But don't expect his thoughts to be profound. What kind of thoughts would you expect from mud and clay? And yet *we* are made of dust and return to dust, so who knows?'

When Rabbi Loewe had finished shaping the Golem,

Jan looked at the large, clumsy figure curiously.

'What happens now?' he asked.

'The giving of life,' replied the Rabbi, drawing a small slip of metal from his pouch. Examining it in the glow of the lantern, Jan saw that it was engraved with Hebrew letters.

'Can you read this word?' asked the Rabbi.

'Yes.'

'What does it say?'

'Emeth.'

'And what does "Emeth" mean?'

'Truth.'

The rabbi bound the metal strip to the Golem's forehead with a piece of cord. Watching fascinated, Jan thought he saw the giant's eyelids flutter.

'And if I remove the first letter from "Emeth",' continued the Rabbi, 'what will it read then?'

'Meth.'

'And what does "Meth" mean?'

'Death.'

'When the time comes for the Golem to die,' Rabbi Loewe went on, 'I shall remove the first letter, and he will once more dissolve into mud. But now he is flesh. Look!' The Rabbi triumphantly lifted his lantern to the giant's face to reveal that it was now the face of a living man. The eyes opened, and to Jan they looked strangely innocent and childlike in the rough, bearded face. But the body and limbs were heavily muscled, those of a man of great strength. Slowly, the giant sat up and looked around him.

'Who am I?' he asked at last, and his voice was deep and harsh.

'You are Yossel the Golem,' replied the Rabbi. 'You were made to serve us.' Then, turning towards the pile of huge garments, he asked Jan to help him dress the giant, which - due to the Golem's size and clumsiness - was less easy than it looked.

'I asked my tailor to make these,' explained the Rabbi, as he and Jan dragged the breeches over the giant's vast legs. 'I told him they were for a poor man I knew who was of exceptional size, and I suppose, in a way, that was true.'

At last the Golem was fully dressed, even down to the boots and the hat, whose heavy brim conveniently concealed the metal strip on his brow. The clothes made him look more like an ordinary man, though an especially large and ugly one.

'What shall we do with him now?' asked Jan.

'I want him to stay in the attic tonight,' replied the Rabbi. 'Tomorrow, after morning service, I shall bring him home to the family, but for now I shall put him to sleep.'

Jan watched, a little apprehensively, as Rabbi Loewe removed the metal strip from the giant's forehead and returned it to his pouch. To Jan's relief the Golem did not disintegrate into mud again, but merely fell asleep, slumped on a pile of prayer-shawls. The noise of his snoring filled the attic.

'Come,' said Rabbi Loewe, and Jan followed him reluctantly down the narrow staircase and into the street. He would have preferred to stay and watch the Golem sleeping.

Later, back in his own downy bed, Jan thought happily about all the miracles the day had held. First there had been his own journey into the past, and then the creation of the Golem. Tomorrow the giant would meet the other inhabitants of the ghetto, and Jan wondered how they would react to each other It had been a long time, he thought, since he had last looked forward to the morning.

It seemed an equally long time before he finally fell asleep.

Jan slept late, and when he woke sunlight was

struggling through the tiny window of his bedchamber. He realized that someone was tapping on his door, and when he answered a giggling maidservant came in, carrying a basin of steaming water, a slab of greyish-looking soap, and something else that Jan assumed was a towel.

As he washed he felt guilty, knowing that someone else had been obliged to draw his water from a well and heat it in a cauldron over a blazing fire. When he had finished, he wondered what he was supposed to do with the dirty water, but the maid soon solved that problem by tipping it out of the window into the street.

As soon as he had dressed, Jan went downstairs to the parlour, there to be confronted by a strange sight. The Golem was seated in the biggest chair, surrounded by the Rabbi's family and servants, who were staring at him with a mixture of awe and amusement, while he stared back with a puzzled air. The Rabbi looked up as Jan entered, and said, 'Ah, Yankel, you see that my household and my Golem have already become good friends. I wish I could say the same about my congregants. When I brought him home from the synagogue after morning prayers several of them followed us in the street, making unflattering remarks about his appearance. They are not as kind as my own family.'

'Couldn't you have made him better-looking, Rabbi?' retorted Jiri, the Rabbi's manservant, while the others laughed. 'Couldn't you at least have made him look like an honest Christian?'

'But he's Jewish, isn't he, Rabbi?' asked Jan.

'Not he,' replied the Rabbi. 'The Golem is a Gentile.'

'Then why do you call him Yossel, if he's not a Jew?'

'Why do *you* have a Gentile name when you *are* a Jew? I gave him a Jewish name so that, having no family of his own, he might feel like a member of our family.'

'So you really love him, after all,' thought Jan. 'Why don't you show it, then?' Aloud, he asked, 'Has he had

44

anything to eat?'

'What, *him*?' snorted Josefina, the fat cook, scornfully. 'What would be the use of stuffing his clay guts with good food?'

'Don't be unkind, Josefina,' said the Rebbetzin before Jan could speak. 'Poor creature, he must eat. And so must you, Yankel,' she added, waving a hand in the direction of the table, which was set with a big brown loaf, cheese, butter, honey, and a flagon of ale.

Jan cut a slice of the loaf, spread it with butter and honey, and held it to the Golem's mouth. Looking puzzled, the giant allowed his tongue to explore the bread. Then he closed his eyes and licked his lips, and a look of sheer pleasure spread over his face.

'He's not such a fool after all,' said the Rabbi, laughing.

Jiri now filled a mug with ale and gave it to the Golem, who drank some and then spat it out in disgust.

'Clever Yossel,' said Jan approvingly. 'Here, have some more bread and honey.'

'Now that you've taught him to eat I expect he'll eat us out of house and home,' snapped Josefina. 'What are his duties going to be, Rabbi? Is he to live in the kitchen with the servants? I don't fancy going about my business with that great image staring at me.'

'His everyday duties will be the usual household ones - chopping wood, drawing water, stoking fires, cleaning the floors,' replied the Rabbi. 'As for his most important duty ... I hope the day will never come when he needs to fulfil it, but we must be prepared.'

The rest of the day passed very enjoyably for Jan, who spent most of his time with the Golem, talking to him, teaching him how to do the household chores that Josefina, Jiri and Marja the maid were too proud to discuss with him, and introducing him to various kinds of food and drink. The Rabbi's family were also kind to Yossel. The Rebbetzin showed him how to churn butter;

Varealina invited him to hold her tapestry wool while she wound it, and the Rabbi tried to teach him the Hebrew alphabet. But it was to Jan's face that Yossel's wide eyes kept straying. 'You and I ... we belong together,' thought Jan. 'We're both strangers.'

When darkness came, Rabbi Loewe suggested that the Golem should once again sleep in the synagogue attic. 'Soon he will have to start guarding the ghetto at night,' he said. 'but I think he should get used to the community, and the community to him, before we turn him loose in the streets alone.'

'May I stay with him, Rabbi?' asked Jan eagerly.

'You? In the attic? All night long?'

'I want to keep him company.'

'But he will go to sleep at once,' said the Rabbi. 'As soon as I remove the formula.'

'Couldn't I remove the formula? When he wants to sleep?'

Rabbi Loewe looked at Jan in bewilderment.

'I don't understand,' he said at last. 'You have just spent an entire day with the creature. Why do you want to spend the night with him as well, in a dusty attic, when you have a comfortable bed to sleep in?'

'It's because I once slept alone in an attic. I know what it feels like.'

The Rabbi patted Jan's shoulder.

'You're a good boy, Yankel,' he said, 'and you teach us all a lesson. Very well, I shall trust you with the Golem and the formula, but see that you bring them both home unharmed.'

So it was that Jan found himself back in the dark attic where the Golem had been created. Yossel looked around fearfully, and clutched Jan's hand.

'I don't like it here,' he said. 'There are eyes looking at me.'

'Those aren't eyes ... they're just spots of moonlight,'

said Jan soothingly. 'They won't hurt you.'

'I'm frightened. Have *you* ever been frightened?'

'Yes. I've been frightened.'

'Talk to me. Tell me about your mother and father, and your sisters. '

So Jan again told the Golem the tales he had been telling him all day, about his family and friends and his old life in the new Prague. Sometimes the Golem laughed; at other times he seemed sad. Then, suddenly, he said, 'Why can't *I* remember?'

'Remember what?' asked Jan.

'The time before this. When *I* had a father and a mother.'

'But you never did ... ' Jan began, and then broke off, not knowing how to continue.

'What *is* a mother?' the Golem asked next.

'Someone who makes you.'

'Rabbi Loewe made me. Is he my mother?'

'No,' replied Jan, close to giggling at the thought of the stern, bearded Rabbi Loewe being anyone's mother. 'The Rabbi is a man. Mothers are women.'

'I'm tired now. I want to sleep.'

Somewhat relieved, for *he* was also feeling tired, Jan took the metal strip from the Golem's forehead. Yossel's eyes closed, and he slumped to the floor and at once began to snore.

Lying beside him on the prayer-shawls, Jan wondered what the Golem was dreaming about. Not very much, probably. His mind was so empty, what could his dreams be like?

When he finally fell asleep, his head on Yossel's shoulder, Jan's own dreams were of his family, lost in an unknown land.

5

The next few days were difficult ones for Jan. Keeping his origins hidden from Rabbi Loewe's family, servants and friends created endless problems. He had to watch both his tongue and his actions, to talk as little as possible, and try to prevent his fingers from fumbling for electric-light switches on the walls and matches in the kitchen. Mistakes had to be explained away by pretending that things were different in his home town of Brno. When a dinner guest asked if he had ever heard of an explorer named Christopher Columbus, he began to reply that he had once seen a film about him at his local cinema, and bit on his tongue just in time. On another occasion he absent-mindedly asked for a fork, and was surprised to see the Rabbi's family gazing at him wide-eyed.

'Surely you don't eat with forks in Brno?' asked the Rebbetzin. 'I thought such luxuries were for the Emperor and his courtiers, not for humble folk like us.' And Jan had to cover his embarrassment with a fit of coughing.

His most awkward moment came on the day the Rebbetzin told him that Josefina was making blanc-mange for dinner. Jan looked forward to the meal eagerly. But when the blancmange arrived, it was not the shivery, pink, strawberry-flavoured concoction he remembered from nursery teas and birthday parties, but a large bowl of a greyish mixture that looked depressing and tasted disgusting.

'What is it?' he gasped, after choking on his first mouthful. 'It ... it tastes of fish.'

'Of course it does,' replied the Rebbetzin mildly. 'It's *made* of fish. Minced fish boiled with milk of almonds, and well seasoned with salt and sugar and ginger and garlic. Isn't that how everyone makes blancmange?'

'Not in Brno,' replied Jan quickly. '*Our* blancmange is pink and floppy. And sweet.'

'It sounds like Mistress Maisl,' giggled Varealina.

'Indeed, Mistress Maisl *is* pink and floppy,' agreed the Rabbi. 'But not especially sweet.'

The Rebbetzin sighed.

'How strange,' she said. 'One would think Brno was on the other side of the moon, instead of a few days' journey from Prague.'

While he tried to keep his own world hidden from his new friends, Jan came to know more about theirs. During the next few days he learned that the ghetto was a walled city alongside the two separate walled cities of Greater and Lesser Prague. The ghetto city towered above the others because the Jewish community, being cramped for space, had to build its houses high, one rickety storey above another like houses of cards. He learned that the ghetto was run by a Jewish Council, and that it had its own Jewish guilds for butchers, goldsmiths, tailors and shoemakers, as well as its own schools, hospital and public baths. And he learned that it was not only the men in the ghetto who wore the equivalent of the Nazi-enforced yellow star, but that the stripes on the bonnets which the women wore for synagogue services also denoted Jewishness - blue stripes for married and yellow stripes for unmarried women. When Jan told Rabbi Loewe about the 'Jude' badges of his own Prague, the Rabbi wrung his hands.

'What, are Jews still wearing yellow badges four hundred years from now?' he lamented. 'Has mankind

49

learned nothing? It seems, Yankel, that your time has more need of the Golem than mine.'

Then he told Jan that the Prague ghetto, which in the not-too-distant past had witnessed massacres and book-burnings, riots and expulsions, was at that time enjoying a rare period of peace and prosperity under the benevolent rule of the Emperor Rudolf II. Jewish festivals were being celebrated openly - the feast of Purim, for example, had recently been marked by a fair, street decorations, strolling players and jesters, and a Lord of Misrule to organize the festivities. As for Mordecai Maisl, the richest man in the ghetto, whom Jan had already glimpsed in the flesh, stout and resplendent in black velvet trimmed with gold - he actually served the Emperor as Minister of Finance, creating a living link between the Court and the Jews.

'If it were not for those accursed friars - may God forgive me for speaking thus about men of religion - we would have nothing to fear,' added the Rabbi, 'and I could have left our friend Yossel in the mud of the river. But *they* still hate us and seek to destroy us. Each Easter, each Passover, it happens - a priest or friar incites the people to believe that Jews kill Christian children for ritual purposes, and then someone leaves a mutilated corpse in the ghetto, and the result is always death for us; either by the gallows or the mob. It happened last year, and it will happen again soon, unless Yossel the Golem can prevent it.'

'Where does the corpse come from?' asked Jan curiously.

'We don't ask such questions. There are dead children enough in Prague. They die by accident, or from beatings. Those men who are wicked enough to use their bodies for such a purpose may even kill them deliberately. There are still wicked men in this world, Yankel.'

'In my world too,' said Jan. 'But there are good people as well.' Then he told Rabbi Loewe how the Nazis had

50

tried to revive the blood ritual accusation, and how the people of his own Prague had refused to believe it.

'So mankind *has* learned something after all?' replied the Rabbi. 'We will survive, then, Yankel ... we will survive. But in the meantime, we must be wary.'

Rabbi Loewe's warning proved well-founded. The people of the ghetto were in the middle of their preparations for Passover - cleaning their houses and strewing the floors with fresh rushes, washing their table and bed-linen, and baking the matzos - when the strangers arrived. A tall man in friar's robes, carrying a crucifix, his eyes blazing with hatred, burst into the Old-New Synagogue one morning while the congregation was at prayer. At his heels followed a crowd of noisy supporters, some twenty or thirty in all, carrying not crucifixes but sticks, staves and stones with which to punish the Jewish 'unbelievers' if they resisted.

'Good-day to you, Rabbi,' said the friar, with a mocking little bow towards the pulpit where Rabbi Loewe stood. 'May I have the honour of preaching in your synagogue this morning?'

'As you please, Father Alois,' replied the Rabbi quietly. Then, as Jan watched in astonishment, he stepped down from the pulpit, seated himself in his throne-like wooden chair, and looked on impassively as the friar planted his crucifix firmly before the Ark and mounted into the pulpit. The rest of the congregation also watched the spectacle without moving or speaking. It occurred to Jan that they were all going through a familiar ritual, a kind of play that they had seen acted out many times before.

Father Alois began to preach, his voice growing ever louder and his face redder as he cursed the Jews for holding fast to their ancestral faith. He accused them of crucifying Christ, of practising idolatrous rituals, and of killing a Christian child at Passover so as to use his blood in the matzos. Each time he stopped for breath, his supporters cheered, hissed, and waved their sticks and stones threateningly.

Jan now realized where he had seen and heard such hatred before. It was in Nazi-occupied Prague; in the speeches of Hitler, heard in broadcasts before his family's radio was confiscated; in the eyes of the SS officers swaggering in the street; in the mocking laughter of the Nazis who had stolen his mother's jewellery and Pavlina's birthday cake. And the silent acquiescence of the people now sitting in the Old-New Synagogue was like the silent acquiescence of his own family and friends. 'Jews don't seem to change much over the centuries,' thought Jan. 'We accept it all so quietly. Why don't we ever hit back?'

When Father Alois had finished his vicious sermon, he spat on the floor, and all his followers promptly followed suit. Then he seized his crucifix and waved it in the air, bowed mockingly once more to Rabbi Loewe, and marched out of the synagogue, his henchmen crowding at his heels, hooting, laughing, and pushing or hitting out at anyone who happened to be standing in their way.

When they had gone, Rabbi Loewe again ascended his pulpit and went on with the service as if nothing extraordinary had happened.

'But why did nobody stop them?' asked Jan later that day, when the Rabbi's family, joined by several of his children and grandchildren, were sitting at dinner.

'Stop them?' replied the Rabbi's only son, Bezalel, in bitter tones. 'That is not allowed. We are not allowed even to protest. They have the right to do as they please with us. They are men of God, and we are only Jews.'

'But they spat on the floor,' protested Jan.

'Yossel can clean up the synagogue,' replied the Rabbi calmly. 'We're lucky that it's only spittle. Last year it was much worse.'

'Poor little Reb Shloime had to clean it last year,' said the Rabbi's daughter Vogele, laughing. 'This year he can at least rest his rheumaticky knees while the Golem does the work.'

'Is *that* why you made him, Father?' asked Tela, another of the Rabbi's daughters. 'To clean spittle from the synagogue floor?'

'Oh no, he cleans *our* floors as well,' replied the Rebbetzin. '*And* chops wood, and stokes the fires, and gets under Josefina's feet. *She* hates him.'

'I did not make him just to be a kitchen menial,' said the Rabbi. 'He has a more important task. You will know what it is tomorrow.'

'Where is he today?' asked Bezalel.

'Sleeping. He rests on the Sabbath.'

'I want to play with the Golem ... I like his face,' mumbled Vogele's little daughter through a mouthful of marzipan, and the Rabbi joined in the laughter.

When the Golem, aroused from his Sabbath sleep, came back to the house that evening, Rabbi Loewe called him into his study, and the two of them sat alone together for some time. After Yossel finally left the Rabbi's presence and came stumping into the kitchen, he seemed to have grown even taller.

'Tomorrow you will love me,' he said to Josefina, turning to wink slyly at Jan, who was helping to peel the vegetables for the evening meal. 'Tomorrow I will be good. The Rabbi told me. Everyone will love me. You will see.'

'I'll wait till tomorrow to believe *that*,' snorted the cook. 'And in the meantime, I suppose you'll be wanting to eat.'

'Everybody eats,' said Jan reasonably.

'Now don't you interfere. Our good Rabbi and Rebbetzin feed everyone, deserving and undeserving, but nobody eats as much as *that* creature does.' Josefina glared at Yossel, who had helped himself to a huge meat

53

pie and a honey cake and was munching them alternately.

He had finished these delicate morsels, and had just turned his attention to the chickens that were roasting on the spits, when the Rabbi suddenly appeared in the kitchen. There was a conspiratorial look on his face, and he beckoned to Yossel, who got up and meekly followed him.

'Thank God,' said Josefina, wiping her brow with a floury hand. 'I don't know where the Rabbi is sending him, but I hope it's a long way from my kitchen.'

Jan did not stop to hear any more. Something exciting was about to happen, and he wanted to see it. Hurrying out of the kitchen, he reached the door of the Rabbi's study just in time to witness a strange sight. The Rabbi stood facing the Golem, holding something resembling an amulet on a long chain between his lifted hands. His family stood watching, all of them, even the lively little grandchildren, frozen in silence and wonder.

'Now you know your duty,' said the Rabbi gravely to the Golem, 'and you will not fail us. So kneel, Yossel, and bend your head.'

The Golem knelt on the floor. Even when kneeling he was taller than the stately Rabbi Loewe. Standing on tiptoes, and lifting his arms as high as they could reach, the Rabbi slipped the amulet and chain around Yossel's neck.

Jan pinched himself, and rubbed his eyes. For the Golem had vanished. Where he had been there was emptiness. Then out of the air, a disembodied but familiar voice said, 'I'm going now, Master.'

'And may the Lord God of Israel keep you,' replied the Rabbi calmly.

Jan, looking around, saw shock and disbelief on the faces of the Rabbi's family. Varealina giggled nervously, and the younger grandchildren began to cry. Then

Bezalel said, 'You've never made anyone invisible before, Father. How did you do it?'

'I found my formula in the pages of the Cabbalah,' replied the Rabbi. 'Have I not told you that nothing in this world is impossible, with God's help?'

As he spoke, the door of the study swung open, and Jan sensed that someone had passed through. Then heavy footsteps sounded in the corridor outside. As if by a signal, all the onlookers, led by the Rabbi, followed the invisible presence. The front door slowly opened, and the chill and darkness of the night air seeped into the house.

'Where have you sent him, husband?' asked the Rebbetzin, wrapping her shawl more tightly round her shoulders, and shivering.

'In search of those evil men who even now may be depositing a dead Christian child in our ghetto,' replied the Rabbi in a grim voice. 'And if he finds nothing tonight, I will send him out again tomorrow, or the next day, or the day after that.'

Standing transfixed, Jan heard the mighty footsteps echo along the cobbled street and then fade into the night.

Next morning the Golem came back empty-handed. He had searched all the alleys and courtyards, he said, and found nothing. Josefina was triumphant.

'I always said he was a stupid good-for-nothing,' she declared. 'Now perhaps the Rabbi will send him packing.'

But the rest of the household was kinder, the Rabbi reassuring the doleful Yossel that the failure of his mission was not his fault. The same thing happened on the next night, and this time the Rebbetzin was puzzled. 'Is *nobody* plotting mischief this Easter?' she asked.

'Wait and see,' replied the Rabbi wisely.

On the third night the Golem again put on his

amulet and went out, invisible, into the chilly darkness. His footsteps died away between the tall, angular houses, and the Rabbi's household went to bed.

Next morning, just after dawn, they were woken by a great clatter in the street, and the sound of booming laughter and terrified screams. Flinging wide his shutters and thrusting his head out of the window, Jan saw a miraculous sight. Suspended in mid-air, as though supported by invisible arms, was a man whom Jan recognized as one of the most vicious of Father Alois's henchmen. It was he who was screaming, his face ashen with fear. Tied to his waist by his own belt was the sagging body of a small boy, stained with blood and limp as a doll. As this macabre couple floated high above the street without any visible support, the laughter boomed out again, and Jan recognized Yossel's voice.

'Have I done well, Master?' shouted the Golem, and the entire family tumbled down into the street to congratulate him.

'I found him in a courtyard,' said Yossel proudly. 'He was putting this poor boy there. He didn't see me. What shall I do with him now, Master? Shall I throw him in the river, or shall I toss him over the rooftops?'

The man moaned with fear, and Rabbi Loewe laughed.

'Neither, Yossel,' he replied. 'I want you to take him, together with his victim, to the house of the Chief Magistrate of Prague. Not in the ghetto ... in the main city. Can you do that, Yossel?'

'I can do anything, Master.'

Meanwhile the wooden shutters all along the street were opening, and astonished faces were peering out of the rows of windows. When they saw what was happening, the neighbours quickly pulled on cloaks over their nightclothes and ran into the street. As the news quickly spread round the tangled alleys of the ghetto, more and more people arrived, until an eager crowd had collected outside the Rabbi's house. Among them Jan recognized Reb Shloime, the meek little beadle of the synagogue, whose cleaning tasks Yossel had inherited.

'It's the Golem ... he's invisible,' somebody shouted, and the crowd began to clap and cheer and dance with joy. Many of them even trailed after Yossel as he bore his trophies towards the ghetto's main gateway.

'If we had bells in the ghetto,' remarked the Rabbi with a smile, 'they would be ringing even now. As for Yossel, I hope he reaches the Chief Magistrate's house without getting lost.'

It was several hours before the Golem returned, full of stories about the sensation his invisible presence had created in the main city. Women had screamed and fainted, and even men had looked pale, he said, as the villain and his dead victim had floated, almost level with the pointed rooftops, towards the Chief Magistrate's house. It had been a day to remember.

'And I hope it will change our history,' said the Rabbi as he removed the amulet from the Golem's neck. 'I think no one will dare to accuse us of ritual murder any more.'

But for Yossel, the greatest triumph of the day was yet to come. Josefina suddenly came running out of the kitchen, seized the Golem's hand, and covered it with kisses.

'Welcome home, dear Yossel!' she cried. 'I've a great feast for you in the kitchen. I've made your favourite quince pie. Will you come and eat?'

As he turned to follow Josefina, a smile appeared on Yossel's huge face. It was the first time anyone had seen him smile.

'I told you everyone would love me,' he said.

During the next few days, Yossel the Golem remained everyone's favourite. Synagogue worthies - including the magnificent Mordecai Maisl - came to inspect and congratulate him, and Josefina continued to be affable. Marja the maid curtseyed and giggled nervously whenever she saw Yossel, and even Jiri went out of his way to be polite to him. Yossel himself strutted about the ghetto like a king.

At first, Jan felt delighted for the Golem, but soon uneasy thoughts began to trouble him. More and more he found himself thinking about the Nemecs, his kind benefactors, and wondering what had happened to them. Had the Gestapo taken them away? They might be suffering on his behalf, Jan told himself, even while *he* was rejoicing with the Golem and enjoying the kindness and hospitality of Rabbi Loewe's house.

The golden bird, still safely hidden in his pocket, now seemed to reproach him whenever he looked at it. The ruby eyes stared back at him accusingly; the outstretched wings that had brought him to Rabbi Loewe's Prague were ready now, it seemed, to take him home again.

It was time for him to go.

Sadly, Jan tapped at the door of Rabbi Loewe's study. The Rabbi looked up with a kindly smile as the boy entered. The walls of the study were lined from ceiling to floor with books, scrolls and manuscripts. It was here that the Rabbi received friends, scholars and petitioners, but now he sat alone, writing with a quill pen on a roll of vellum. He was working, Jan knew, on his new book, a commentary on Judaism called 'The Way of Life'. Papers were scattered about, on his desk and on the floor, and the room smelled of guttering candles and crackling logs and old parchment. Jan wished he could stay there for ever.

'Ah, Yankel,' said the Rabbi. 'Have you heard? All Prague is talking about our Yossel. Master Maisl tells me that the Emperor himself has asked to see him. Can you imagine Yossel as a courtier? I shall have to order some splendid new clothes for him. A hat with a feather,

58

perhaps?'

'I wish I could stay long enough to see him wear them,' said Jan sadly.

'But why should you not stay?' asked the Rabbi in surprise. 'This is your home now.'

'No, Rabbi. My home is where my family and my friends are.'

Then, encouraged by the Rabbi's silence and his enquiring look, Jan began to speak. He spoke of his guilt, the debt he owed the Nemec family, and his longing to know if they were safe. When he had finished, the Rabbi said, 'Of course you must go, Yankel. We would be selfish if we kept you here.'

'Not selfish, Rabbi. These have been wonderful days. I shall never forget them.'

'And you will know wonderful days again in your own time, when the tyrant is vanquished,' said the Rabbi. 'The days of persecution passed for us, and they will also pass for you, God willing. But if they should not ...'

'If they should not?'

'Then come back to us. Keep hold of your golden bird, and come back. You will always have a home and friends here.'

'I know. May God reward you, Rabbi.'

Now that he had made up his mind, Jan decided to leave at once. He explained to the Rabbi's household that he had decided to go back to Brno to see if any of his relatives or friends had survived the pogrom. Then, with the Rabbi's blessing and the Rebbetzin's lamentations in his ears he left the house and ran down the cobbled street, not daring to look back until he had reached the cemetery.

The graveyard, still strangely new and small and unfamiliar to his eyes, lay drowsing in the gilded evening light. He crouched on the grass beside one of the stones, and took the golden bird out of his pocket. The ruby eyes watched him expectantly.

'Take me back,' said Jan boldly, stroking the bird's golden wings. 'I wish I was back in my own time.'

This time Jan knew what to expect. As the dizziness enveloped him, and then the darkness, he closed his eyes and waited. The dizziness soon subsided and he opened his eyes, half dreading what he was going to see.

The cemetery had grown large again, and immensely old. In the long, tangled grasses the ancient stones lay tumbled, slanting against the evening sky, their carvings and inscriptions faded with age. Facing him was a large sarcophagus, carved with lions, its inscription informing the world that this was the last resting-place of the miraculous Rabbi Judah Loewe ben Bezalel, who had departed this life in the year 1609.

Tears filled Jan's eyes. For a moment he paused, caressing the faded stone as if he were caressing the Rabbi's kindly bearded face. Then, rubbing his eyes with his fists, he left he cemetery and retraced his steps towards Hitler's Prague.

6

Jan did not hurry. If he waited long enough and all went
well, he told himself, Mr Nemec would be home from
work and the children from school, and the Gestapo
would have returned to the flat, found nothing and gone
away again. If all had *not* gone well, then there was time
enough for him to know.

But what was the time? And what day was it? What
month, or year? Had any time actually elapsed between
his journey to Rabbi Loewe's Prague and his return?
Might he reach Wenceslas Square to find the Czech flag
flying again over the tall buildings, Hitler gone, and the
world grown older and more civilized? Jan's heart beat
faster, caught between hope and fear.

But of course it was all too much to hope for. Jan had
not walked far before he saw the swastikas again, the
Hitler portraits sneering from shop-fronts, the Nazi
soldiers in shiny boots and armbands watching from
doorways as Czech citizens trod the pavements warily.
In the medieval ghetto, although the Jews were a
despised minority, there had been a feeling of warmth
and kinship, thought Jan. Here a chill wind blew. He
shivered.

Stopping to peer at a headline as he passed a newspaper kiosk, Jan noticed that the date had not altered.
His visit to Old Prague had been a leap out of time,
leaving no mark on his present existence. Jan walked
past the grand facade of the National Museum and
turned off towards the quiet side street where the

Nemecs lived.

He slowed down as he approached the house. The moment had come, and he was afraid. All at once he remembered that Mrs Nemec had warned him to stay away for several days. But it was too late to turn back now. The heavy front door loomed up before him and he pressed the Nemecs' bell with a trembling finger.

Nobody answered.

It was too soon, thought Jan desperately. Or perhaps they had not heard him. Perhaps the bell was not working. He pressed it again, this time more firmly.

By the time he had rung half a dozen times, Jan knew. But he had to be sure. He rang the bell of the flat downstairs. There was a short pause, and then the door opened slowly, and a woman's anxious face appeared. Jan recognized her as the neighbour who had warned Mrs Nemec of the Gestapo's visit. He had sometimes spoken to her in earlier, happier days.

She knew him now, for her eyes widened in dismay.

'It's you!' she said in a low voice. 'What are you doing back here? Haven't you done enough damage?'

'Where are the Nemecs?' asked Jan, his voice trembling.

'*You* should know. They took them away. The Gestapo. They came back about an hour ago, and took them all away.'

'Where to?'

'How should *I* know? A concentration camp, probably.'

'But why?' cried Jan. 'There was no one there. *I* wasn't there.'

'You didn't have to be. The accusation was enough. They were taken away on suspicion of harbouring Jews.'

'But that isn't fair ...'

'Don't you know *anything*?' hissed the woman angrily. 'Don't you know better than to stand here? Anybody could be watching. *I* could be arrested myself

62

for talking to you.'

'But ...'

'Go away.'

And she slammed the door in his face.

Jan knew now what he had to do. He was tired of hiding, tired of running away. The golden bird could have taken him back to Rabbi Loewe's Prague, and he could have stayed there for ever. But it seemed too easy. Others had suffered on his behalf, and now it was his turn.

Besides, he longed to see his family again. If he gave himself up to the Gestapo, he would be sent to Terezin and reunited with his mother, Grandpa, and Pavlina and Monika. Terezin might even be a pleasant place ... Grandpa had said so. But first he must see his old home again, if only for a few moments. He needed to know who was living there now.

As he turned towards Krizovnicka Street, Jan felt a surge of excitement. He had not seen the house for more than a year, and now he looked forward to standing once more in the spacious rooms where he had spent his lovely childhood.

The outside of the building seemed unchanged. Jan pressed the doorbell firmly. The family name, he noticed, had vanished from the bell-push, to be replaced by the name 'Dortmund'. Jan wondered what the Dortmunds were like.

After a few moments the door opened. A man stood in the doorway, eyeing Jan curiously. He was tall and fair-haired, and wore SS uniform. His jackboots gleamed, and there was a swastika band round his arm.

'Yes?' he said tersely.

'I used to live here,' replied Jan, and the man drew in his breath sharply.

'Your name is Weiss?' he asked.

'Yes.'

63

'Come inside,' said the man, grabbing Jan by the arm and drawing him into the corridor. The door closed behind them, and for a moment Jan panicked. Then he remembered the golden bird deep in his pocket, and felt reassured. There was no need to be afraid, he thought, with escape always at hand.

Still holding Jan's arm firmly, the man led him along the familiar corridor and into the dining-room.

The room was the same, and yet different. The furniture was unchanged, and so were the carpets and curtains, but a portrait of Hitler smiled his evil smile from the wall where pictures of Jan's Jewish great-grandparents had once hung. Framed photographs of men in Nazi uniform stood on the sideboard alongside Mother's treasured Venetian glass vase. Jan noticed that a woman, seated at the table, was pouring coffee from Grandma's coffee-pot, and that a little girl with blond pigtails was playing with Pavlina's dolls'-house. He wanted to shout, 'Leave them alone - they're not yours!' but his tongue seemed to freeze in his mouth.

'Who's this?' asked the woman, looking up from her coffee-cups.

'A little Jewboy,' replied the man scornfully. 'This is Master Weiss, who used to live here. Evidently he escaped the transports.'

The little girl screwed up her face as if she were smelling something nasty.

'Oh, Daddy, is he a Jew? How horrible!' she said. 'Make him go away!'

'Not till I've asked him a few questions,' her father replied. 'Now tell me, Master Weiss, where have you been hiding? And who has been hiding you?'

Jan did not reply.

'That's not important, Hansi,' said the woman. 'The important thing is to get rid of him.'

'So you won't talk?' asked the man, ignoring her and looking at Jan angrily. 'Very well, perhaps you'll talk to my friends in the Gestapo.' And he went to the telephone and dialled a number.

Jan should have been terrified, and yet for some reason he felt only defiance. While the man spoke on the telephone in a harsh, rasping German, Jan stood staring at the woman and the little girl, who stared back at him blankly. His eyes roamed to the delicious-looking cakes on the table, and he suddenly found himself wishing that the woman would offer him one.

Jan spent that night in an exhibition hall on the outskirts of Prague, together with a small group of captured Jews like himself. The Gestapo officer who had arrived in response to Herr Dortmund's angry telephone call was not nearly as fearsome as he had expected. He did not take Jan to Gestapo headquarters or interrogate him, but merely put him in a van and drove him in silence to the collection-point. It seemed he spent much of his time rounding up stray Jews, and found the task boring. Jan's main emotion, as he left Krizovnicka Street, was anger that the Dortmunds felt no guilt at having stolen his family's home and possessions.

About fifty Jews, all adults, were gathered in the exhibition hall when Jan arrived. It was a bare, echoing place, without beds or any other furniture, and Jan and his new friends had to sleep that night on the dusty floor. But they were fed on bread, coffee and cabbage soup, and provided with sinks to wash in. Better still, none of the German guards abused or ill-treated them. Jan lay down on his coat and tried to make himself as comfortable as he could.

'I suppose things could be worse,' said a middle-aged man who had introduced himself to Jan as a former lawyer. 'I've been here three days, and nothing has happened, except that they keep bringing in more people.'

'Where do they come from?' asked Jan.

'They've been hiding in the forest, or in cellars, or with non-Jewish friends,' replied the man. 'Most people get rounded up in the end. My own family was taken away with the first transports.'

'So was mine,' replied Jan, feeling an odd sense of kinship with this portly man with the balding head and dignified manner.

By the time the group left Prague next morning, Jan had become friendly with most of its members and knew their histories. The women were especially kind and motherly towards him, having seen their own children taken away. Like him, they were hoping for a happy reunion with their families in Terezin.

'But suppose we don't get taken there?' asked Jan, stricken by a sudden fear.

'Don't worry, we will,' said one of the women soothingly. 'I heard a guard say so.'

And so it was that Jan felt almost cheerful when the guards informed the group next morning that they would be leaving that day. Spring sunlight glittered on the rooftops, and Jan found himself enjoying the walk to the railway station. The group, escorted by its Nazi guards, attracted occasional pitying glances from passers-by, but Jan did not feel any need for pity. Soon, he told himself firmly, he would see his family again.

As the party clambered aboard the waiting train, Jan heard a guard say, 'It's a pity to waste a whole train on such a small group, isn't it? *I* would have made them walk.' But it was so long since he had travelled anywhere that he eagerly pressed his nose to the carriage window as the train slid out of the station and into the glowing green countryside.

The journey took about an hour. Fields and forests and blossoming orchards flew by to the thunderous music of the wheels; villages came and went, clusters of grey stone houses with red roofs, and every so often a church lifted its spires and onion domes to the blue sky. Eventually a wide plain appeared, with glimpses of undulating hills, and then came a river, winding gently through vineyards and overhanging trees.

'There it is - that's Terezin!' said one of Jan's companions, pointing, and they all became aware of something on the skyline that looked like a medieval city. As they drew nearer they could make out red and grey roofs, ramparts and battlements, and high walls pierced by massive gates.

'Why, it's like the old Prague ghetto,' thought Jan in amazement. 'It's like Rabbi Loewe's ghetto, except that *he* won't be there.'

Within a few minutes the walled city was looming up before them, and a gate, guarded by policemen, was opening to receive the train.

'We're going right inside,' said one of the women. 'That's good. We won't have to walk far.'

The train was now passing between tall, barrack-like buildings. It seemed to Jan's bemused gaze that a crowd of shadowy figures stood on the sidelines, awaiting them.

The train slid along the track and slowly came to a halt.

7

As the carriage doors opened and Jan and his friends clambered down onto the platform, the shadowy figures surged forward. Seeing them close-to, Jan felt a sudden sense of shock. Not even the refugees he had seen queuing at the Jewish soup kitchen in Nazi Prague had ever looked as hungry, ragged and depressed as these people. Their faces were wan and grey, their skin covered with sores and scabs, and their threadbare clothes hung loosely on their gaunt bodies.

And yet, for all their miserable state, they seemed to be making an effort to be kind and comforting as they welcomed the latest batch of prisoners to Terezin. As the newcomers were led down a long narrow street between the tall grey buildings, the ghostly figures whispered to them reassuringly, urging them not to be frightened, and promising them that everything would be all right.

The group's first stop was at a checkpoint building, where their personal details were taken by uniformed police and their identity cards stamped. They received billet and ration cards, and were medically examined and searched for money and other valuables. At this moment Jan panicked, terrified that his treasured golden bird would be found and taken away. He hid it under his tongue when nobody was looking and, much to his surprise, the ruse worked. Some of the women in the group were wearing jewellery, and most of the other prisoners had money, and nobody seemed to be over-interested in a small boy who apparently possessed neither.

After that, the group was taken to a bath-house, where they took uncomfortable showers, without soap, hot water or proper towels. Then came a visit to the delousing station, where they were doused in a gas-like substance intended, so they were told, to kill fleas. By this time Jan was feeling hungry and exhausted, and he was pleased to hear one of the welcoming party murmur, 'Don't worry, son. It will all be over soon, and then you'll get something to eat.'

With pleasant visions of a meal in his mind, Jan allowed himself to be led to one of the barrack-like buildings which, he was told, would be his new home. He felt rather less reassured when his new guide added, 'A boy called Milos died here last week, so you'll be able to have *his* bunk.'

Jan's first glimpse of the inside of the building did not make him feel any better. It was a sparse, bare place, chilly despite the warm sunshine outside, and the room into which he was led seemed to contain no furniture apart from stacks of narrow bunks. Some of these were obviously occupied, even though it was nearly midday, for as Jan passed the bunks he was aware of weasel-like faces peering out at him with glittering eyes. But not all the children in the room were in bed; some were sitting in a semi-circle on the floor, facing a man who appeared to be their teacher, for he was reading to them out of a battered old book. Occasionally he asked a question, and one of the children would put up his hand to reply. The children, Jan noticed, were all boys, and most were near his own age.

Jan's guide, whose name was Ivo, and who was apparently in charge of the room, led him to an empty bunk with no pillows and only one blanket. Jan wondered if it would feel as uncomfortable as it looked. He glanced up at his escort and nervously asked, 'What did he die of?'

'What did *who* die of?'

'The boy who used to sleep here.'

'Oh, Milos,' replied Ivo in casual tones. 'People die here of all kinds of things. I can't remember what happened to Milos. People are dying all the time.'

'Do the children do lessons?' asked Jan, thinking it might be safer to change the subject.

'Yes, every day,' answered his guide. 'That group over there is a Latin class. Later on today we shall have classes in mathematics and English literature. We try to keep to a normal school curriculum. It's all forbidden, but we do our best.'

'Forbidden? By whom?'

'By the Nazis, of course. The teachers would be punished if they were ever caught teaching the children. But they do it, all the same. They're heroes and hero-ines, every one.'

Not reassured by the answers to his questions so far, Jan thought he would attempt a third. His stomach felt pinched with hunger, and there was no sign as yet of the promised meal.

'Are we going to eat soon?' he asked hopefully.

'As soon as this class is finished. I'll get one of the boys to show you to the children's cook-house. Have you got your ration-card?'

'Yes, sir.'

'Good. Be careful not to lose it, or you'll go hungry.' He smiled wryly, as though he had cracked a rather bitter joke.

Jan was to understand the significance of the smile a little later, when the Latin class was finished and a boy of about his own age, named Evald, was assigned to look after him. Unlike the adults, whose clothes hung loosely on them, the children mostly seemed to have grown out of their threadbare clothes. Evald's shrunken shirt and shorts revealed long, gaunt arms and legs covered with red sores.

'Hurry up,' were his first words to Jan, 'or we'll lose our place in the queue.'

'Which queue?'

'At the cook-house, silly. Look, the others will all get there before us.'

The other children - except for those who seemed too weak to leave their bunks - were indeed surging eagerly out of the building. They now joined a vast mass of other children, girls as well as boys, who had appeared from nowhere and were converging on a long, low hut near the barracks, where the crowd formed itself into a long, snaking queue.

'Where did the other children come from?' whispered Jan to his new friend.

'The other rooms.'

'How long will we have to wait?'

'Oh, at least an hour.'

'An *hour*?' Jan clutched his stomach in dismay. 'I can't wait that long. I'm starving.'

Evald smiled grimly.

'You don't know what it is to starve yet,' he replied. 'Just you wait.'

As the queue inched slowly forward towards the cook-house door, Jan tried to ask Evald more questions, but Evald appeared reluctant to talk. Mostly he replied, 'You'll see' or, 'Just wait.' The children in front of him seemed equally silent. There was none of the usual chatter that had accompanied dinner-time at school.

At last, just as Jan felt he was about to die of hunger, his turn came. He found himself standing at a long counter covered with wooden troughs of bread. A steaming cauldron stood behind the counter, and Jan sniffed and eyed it hungrily as a woman clipped a coupon out of his ration-card. Another woman poured a ladleful of soup from the cauldron into a small bowl, and handed it to Jan together with a hunk of bread.

71

Jan turned to Evald to ask, 'Can we eat it right away?' only to find that Evald was already gobbling his own meal ravenously. Obviously there was no need to wait till they got back to their room. Jan lifted his soup bowl eagerly to his lips, took a gulp, and then winced. It was cabbage soup, and the nastiest he had ever tasted.

'It's horrible,' he spluttered. 'The cabbage must have been bad.'

'It tastes all right to me,' replied Evald, who was already mopping up the last lingering drops of his soup with a piece of bread.

Jan now took a mouthful of bread. It tasted even worse than the soup, and he spat it out in disgust.

'The bread's mouldy again today,' explained Evald kindly. 'It often is. You'll soon get used to the taste.'

'Get used to *that*? Never.'

'The food the grown-ups get is even worse,' said one of the other children. 'The camp Elders save the best food for *us*. Sometimes it's better than this. Today isn't a very good day.'

'You can say that again,' replied Jan.

Evald, having finished his own meal, now turned pleading eyes on Jan's partly eaten bread.

'If you're not going to finish that, can I have it?' he asked.

Jan handed it over slowly, and watched in dismay as Evald began to cram the nauseous stuff eagerly into his mouth as though he were truly starving.

Later that day Jan was able to see something more of his new home. The prisoners, he discovered, were free to move about as they pleased when they were not working. But first he was careful to hide his precious amulet inside his mattress when he was sure that no one was watching. Luckily, there were various holes and slits in the covering, and the golden bird slid easily through one of these into the musty straw filling. Jan replaced the blanket, feeling he had done all he could to safeguard his means of escape.

For the other prisoners, less lucky than himself, no such escape route existed. Jan realized that as soon as he began to explore Terezin. The whole town was like a walled fortress, entirely surrounded by a moat and three belts of ramparts pierced by gates guarded by armed police. There were tall grey barracks everywhere, which loomed over the other buildings. The streets, which were ruler-straight and intersected each other at right angles, were named with numbers and letters - such as L6 and Q8 - painted in black on yellow signboards. And yet Jan was surprised to see that Terezin, within its grim walls, had the general look of a pleasant little country town. Terraced rows of stone houses enclosed small green squares; a church steeple rose from a cloud of foliage; the main square was bordered with trees, and the small block of houses on its edge was surrounded by bright flower gardens. Jan even glimpsed a café and a small parade of shops which appeared to include a post-office and a bookshop. Somewhere in the distance he seemed to hear an invisible orchestra playing a lively waltz - or was it his imagination? His heart leaped, and he began to wonder in which of these small stone houses with the pretty gardens his family was living, and how long it would take them to find each other. Buoyed by hope, he almost forgot his hunger.

A few moments later Jan's heart sank again. A cart had trundled past, drawn by two men, and he noticed with a shiver that it was piled with coffins loosely covered with a black flag emblazoned with a yellow star. Then, as he stood watching, something even more horrible happened. An old woman swathed in a ragged shawl came shuffling out of a side street, stopped, swayed, and fell to the ground. The cart stopped, and one of the men bent over her, listened for her heart-beat, and felt her pulse. Then he said something to the other man, and between them they lifted the old woman onto the stack of coffins as easily as if she had truly been the scarecrow she resembled. One wrinkled arm, thin as a bone, hung down from under the black flag. The men seized the shafts of the cart and, looking totally unconcerned, went on their way.

When Jan next saw Evald he told him in hushed tones what he had seen. 'Oh, that's nothing,' replied Evald casually. 'The coffin cart comes through the camp several times a day. People are dying all the time.'

'Yes, but that poor old lady ... it was so awful ...'

'A lot of old people die,' Evald went on. 'Mostly they die of starvation. They get less food than the rest of us. The Elders give us part of their rations. They're not needed, you see.'

'Not needed? What do you mean?'

'Well, they can't do any work. Most of the adults are at work right now, except for those who are ill. Workers die as well, and so do children, but mostly it's the old people.'

'What happens to the bodies?' asked Jan, trying to sound as casual as his new friend.

'Those coffins you saw were on their way to the crematorium,' replied Evald. 'First, any gold teeth in the bodies will be taken out, and then the bodies will be burned and the ashes scattered in the river.'

'Which river?'

'Didn't you see it when you arrived?'

'Yes, I did,' said Jan, suddenly remembering the peaceful little river, overhung with trees, that he had glimpsed from the train. Then that tranquil image vanished, to be replaced by the image of a cart, a pile of coffins, and a thin arm dangling from under a black flag.

There were things in Terezin, Jan was now beginning to realize, that did not seem to fit together.

Later that day the children again queued for food at their cook-house, and by this time Jan was so ravenous that he ate the mouldy bread without noticing the taste. He had a spoonful of jam as well, and a mug of bitter coffee. To his surprise, he found himself almost enjoying this miserable meal.

At about seven o'clock the adults came back from their work, some from the camp's factories and work-shops and others, in escorted groups, from the fields, orchards and farmyards. There seemed to be thousands of them spilling through the narrow streets towards the cook-houses. Jan watched eagerly for a glimpse of Mother or Grandpa, but there were too many people, and the weary grey faces all seemed to look alike. Sooner or later, Jan promised himself, he would find them.

Meanwhile there were other things to occupy his mind. For a few nightmarish moments Jan thought he could see the old woman's ghost wherever he looked; then he realized that numerous old people, men as well as women, had come out of their houses and were begging for food in the streets. They looked like living skeletons as they shuffled over the cobbles, their hands outstretched in silent pleading. One or two of the work-ers handed over a morsel of food, but most people ignored them. Every so often one of the ghostly figures slumped to the ground and lay there, a crumpled heap of bones and rags, waiting to be collected by the coffin cart. Jan found himself remembering Grandma Freiberg, who had died in a warm comfortable bed, with the doctor calling regularly during her illness, and Mother trying to force chicken soup and jelly between her lips.

But the old people, starving and dying, were not the only terrifying visions encountered by Jan that day. The Nazi guards, appearing every so often out of the shad-ows, and without warning, were worse. Sometimes they merely kicked or beat the prisoners; sometimes they set dogs on them, or shot them for reasons that were not always obvious. Sometimes prisoners were taken away to the prison known as the Small Fortress, and were never seen again. Though the ghetto was run - as Rabbi Loewe's had been - by the Jewish Council, the Nazis had absolute power, and used it. It was they who lived, Jan was told, in the little houses surrounded by pretty flower gardens on the edge of the main square.

As he clambered into his bunk that night, Jan found himself thinking what a place of contrasts this Terezin was turning out to be. He had enjoyed the afternoon lessons and was beginning to make friends among the children in his room, and yet there were things - such as the starving old people, the coffin cart and the cruel Nazi guards - that made him shiver. He whispered a prayer, hoping that the good things would outweigh the bad, and further consoled himself by remembering the golden bird tucked safely away in the dank straw of his mattress.

The bunk was just as uncomfortable as he had expected. Straw poked through the holes in the mattress and scratched his skin, and his blanket felt rough and smelt musty. For some reason he also felt as if a thousand needles were pricking him, and he woke next morning to find his body covered in itchy red bumps.

'It's bedbugs,' explained Evald. 'Bedbugs, fleas and lice. Don't worry. We've all got them.'

'Mother used to say only dirty people caught fleas and lice,' thought Jan ruefully. 'What will she say when she finds out?'

Mother seemed unlikely to find out, at least for the time being. All next day Jan searched the adult faces thronging the ghetto streets, but saw no trace of her. Nor were Monika and Pavlina anywhere to be found. Jan had noticed that the boys and girls in the children's barracks mostly appeared to be about his own age. What, he wondered, had happened to the younger ones?

When Jan next saw Ivo, his room Elder, he asked how to set about finding his family. To his dismay, Ivo laughed bitterly.

'Do you really expect to find anyone in this place?' he asked. 'Do you expect anyone to know anyone here? Do you know how many thousands of people live here? Not to speak of the thousands who have died, and all those other thousands who have passed through?'

'Passed through? What do you mean, sir?' asked Jan, puzzled.

'I'm talking about those people who have been transported East.'

'Transported? I don't understand.'

'Of course not. You're new here.'

Then Ivo explained that people did not necessarily stay in Terezin once they arrived there, and that trains left every so often for a mysterious destination in the eastern territories.

'Most of the younger children are sent East as soon as they get here,' Ivo went on. 'We don't know what awaits them in the East. We prefer not to know.'

Until that moment it had not occurred to Jan that his family might no longer be in Terezin. Now he suddenly realized for the first time that he might never see them again. But before he could ask any more questions, Ivo added, 'You must think of yourself, now, my boy. Everyone owes it to himself to stay alive. I was meaning to ask you ... would you like to work?'

'*Can* I work?' asked Jan miserably.

'If I find you a job,' replied Ivo. 'I've heard they need more workers on the vegetable farm. Part-time, for you, as you're under-age. You look like a strong lad. How old are you?'

'Thirteen and a half.'

'Nearly fourteen?'

Jan nodded.

'Could you pretend to be fifteen?' asked Ivo. Then, as

Jan looked at him in surprise, he added, 'Older is better. You could earn yourself some money, and you could also make yourself useful. It's very important, in this place, to be useful. Well, do you want to work on the farm?'

'Yes, sir. Please.'

So Jan started work early next morning. Roll-call for the workers was at four o'clock, and Jan shivered in the cold dawn air as his party was marched out into the dark, sleeping fields beyond the ghetto, hoes and shovels on their shoulders. His uncomfortable bunk had never looked so tempting, and his empty stomach growled with hunger.

'It's much worse in winter,' a member of his party murmured soothingly. 'Summer is coming, and we can be thankful for that.'

Jan soon learned that there were other things to be thankful for. The police who guarded the field workers, for example, were Czech not German; they treated the prisoners kindly, and let them stop occasionally to rest. The fields smelled fresh and sweet after the stench of the ghetto; there was plenty of space compared with the crowded streets, and the damp earth promised rich harvests as the prisoners dug, scattered seed or transplanted seedlings. After a few hours the workers, now weak with hunger, were given a meal of bread, jam and coffee. Jan ate and drank ravenously, feeling he had earned this feast.

At the end of his first week as a worker, Jan received his wages. The money looked unlike any money he had known in Prague. It was specially-minted coinage - Jewish money - quite useless outside Terezin. But Jan was eager to discover what it would buy inside the camp, and as soon as he had a moment to spare from work and lessons, he and Evald made their way joyfully to the parade of shops on the main square.

'I wonder if there'll be anything decent to eat,' said Evald.

'Chocolate,' gulped Jan.

'Tinned sardines for me,' said Evald. 'I love sardines. I've always wanted to buy some, but I've never had any money.'

The boys need not have hurried. They soon discovered that there was no food in the one and only food shop, apart from mustard and some jars of a mysterious paste. The other shops contained shabby clothes and various other shoddy-looking goods. Yet not all was gloom and despair. Several people were sitting at tables in the little open-air café, sipping a brew that looked like coffee and listening to a small orchestra. The lively music of a polka filled the square.

Jan ordered two cups of coffee, handing over some of his precious coins and the boys sat down at a table and prepared to enjoy themselves.

'Don't you wish there was some cake?' asked Jan.

'Ugh! This coffee is just as disgusting as the stuff we get in the cook-house,' exclaimed Evald angrily. 'This café is a fake. It's not fair! *Everything* in Terezin is a fake.'

'The music isn't a fake,' said Jan, watching the musicians' instruments glinting in the sunlight. The lovely, lilting notes of Smetana's *Bartered Bride* seemed to dance on the spring air.

Jan discovered that the only good things in Terezin that were not fakes were the music and the learning. The lessons in the children's barracks, often given by famous scholars and professors, seemed far more interesting than those he remembered from his schooldays in Prague, and the children were also allowed to attend the adult lectures and discussion groups. But it was the music that made Terezin special. It spilled out every day from the narrow, stinking streets, out of basements and barracks and uncurtained windows: Mozart and Schubert, waltzes and mazurkas and thrilling choral

music. There were many famous musicians and compos-
ers among the prisoners in the ghetto, Ivo explained,
and the musical instruments had been smuggled in
from the outside world.

'But why don't the Nazis stop it?' asked Jan.

'Stop it? They encourage it,' Ivo replied and Jan
stared at him in astonishment.

'Don't you understand *yet*?' Ivo added before Jan
could speak. 'Terezin is a show-camp. The Nazis set it up
on purpose, to show the outside world just how well the
Führer treats the Jews. This place is a paradise compared with the other camps. We have music and art and
drama. We even have a library with thousands of books.
Of course we die like flies from starvation and disease
and beatings, but the important visitors who come here
to inspect the camp don't see those. All they hear is the
music.'

When Jan told Evald what Ivo had said, Evald
nodded.

'That's the only thing I have to thank the Nazis for,'
he said. 'The music. I never heard any music at home.
Did you?'

Once again Jan found himself thinking how strange
it was that Evald should now be his best friend. It
happened only because Evald had been assigned to look
after him on the day he arrived. Back home in Prague
they might never have met. Evald came from a different
background; his parents had sold vegetables from a
market stall. They were both dead now, and so was
Evald's sister. They had all died in the typhoid epidemic
that had swept the camp the previous summer.

'Yes,' Jan replied, a little afraid of being thought
snobbish. 'We used to go to lots of concerts.'

'And the opera?'

'Yes. That too.'

'Well, everything was different with us,' said Evald.
'We never went anywhere. We had a wireless, but my

parents liked music hall and big band shows. I never heard real music till I came here. Did you know that there's even a children's choir? In some ways I wouldn't have missed this place for the world. If only ...' Here Evald broke off, and stared down at the ground.

'If only ...' Jan prompted him.

'If only we weren't afraid all the time. There are things here that would be wonderful, if only we weren't afraid.'

'What are you afraid of most?' asked Jan.

Evald looked surprised.

'The same as everyone else,' he replied. 'Beatings ... hangings ... shootings ... but mostly the transports East.'

Jan, remembering what Ivo had told him, saw an opportunity to find out more. 'What *are* the transports East?' he asked.

'Nobody knows,' replied Evald. 'We're all afraid of the transports, but we don't even know where East *is*. That's what's so frightening.'

Jan looked at his pale face, and felt a sudden surge of fear.

8

Weeks and months passed, and for Jan the worst thing in the camp was still the hunger.

There were other things that *should* have been worse. The coffin carts continued to trundle through the streets, and old people still died in the gutters. Nazi guards still strutted through the ghetto, kicking, punching or shooting innocent passers-by. And then there were the moments of terror nearer home, as when an SS officer made a sudden, unannounced visit to the children's barracks while lessons were in progress. Luckily a boy acting as look-out was always able to warn them in time, so that the forbidden books were hidden under the blankets and the children slumped aimlessly on their bunks before the intruder kicked the door open. His sharp eyes roamed everywhere, and Jan held his breath. When the officer had gone, the teacher - who would have been hanged had he been caught red-handed - went on explaining an algebra problem or reading a Shakespeare sonnet as calmly as if nothing unusual had happened.

Yes, the dangerous moments were frightening, but the hunger was worse still. The hunger could never be forgotten, day *or* night. Sometimes the food was more edible than on other days, and sometimes there were unexpected titbits, but there was never enough. Jan now ate the mouldy bread as ravenously as Evald had done. There were constant gnawing pains in his stom-

82

ach, and his ribs were beginning to show through his skin. During the day he thought endlessly about the lovely meals he had eaten at home in happier days. At night he dreamed about pies and sausages and steaming chicken soup, roast carp, strudel bursting with nuts and raisins, and pastries piled with whipped cream. One night he dreamed it was his birthday and Mother, smiling, was lighting the candles on a magnificent iced cake. Jan woke in tears, not knowing if he was crying for Mother or the cake.

These days he was beginning to give up hope of ever finding her again, even though he still dutifully looked for her face, and those of Grandpa, Monika and Pavlina in the crowded ghetto streets. Sometimes he even found himself wondering whether the search for food was becoming more important to him than the search for his family.

As the summer passed, he began to look forward to the time when the vegetables he and his fellow-workers had planted and tended in the fields would ripen. He watched the tomatoes growing fat and red in the sun, the carrots plump and golden, the radishes crisp, the peas and beans bursting in their pods, the lettuces succulent, and he eyed them greedily. But no sooner had he helped himself to a carrot and eagerly wiped it clean on his sleeve than one of the Czech guards snatched it away. Jan, looking up in dismay, saw that his fellow-workers were watching him with a mixture of amusement and pity.

'Don't you dare touch any of those,' said the guard sharply, 'or we'll all be hanged. These vegetables are for our German masters, not for us.'

'Don't we get *any*?' asked Jan, shocked.

'Not so much as a bean. Not so much as a pea. And don't you forget that.'

'That's not fair ...' Jan began, but an older prisoner silenced him by placing a finger over his mouth.

'Don't you know *anything* yet, lad?' the man murmured in his ear. 'Do you expect things to be fair? *You've* burst your guts digging and planting and hoeing and weeding and watering these lovely fresh vegetables, and now the Nazis will eat them and feed *you* on mouldy cabbage and stinking turnips. No, things won't be fair again till God delivers us from this terrible place!'

As he listened to these words, Jan's heart felt as hollow as his stomach. From that day he loathed his work in the fields; he resented having to harvest the vegetables and load them onto carts, and he tried not to watch as the carts, brimming with good food, were trundled away in the direction of the Nazi officers' kitchens.

The food cooked *there*, Jan knew, was infinitely better than anything provided for the prisoners. One of the older girls in the children's barracks worked there, and it was rumoured that she regularly stole food from the Nazi larders to bring back for the child prisoners. Whenever something edible found its way into their cookhouse, Jan and his friends secretly thanked Anna, who had risked her life to feed them. She was a big, rather bossy girl of fifteen, with dark hair that hung down her back in a heavy plait, and the younger children looked on her as a heroine, for theft was punishable by death. Sometimes Jan worried about her thieving activities. He had always been taught that it was wrong to steal. But when some tasty morsel appeared on his plate, he forgot his scruples.

One day, as Jan stopped to admire the flowers in the gardens of the SS billets, he was dismayed to see a Nazi officer beckoning to him. Jan approached slowly, his feet dragging and his heart thumping, but as he drew closer he was relieved to see that the man, despite his swastika armband and gleaming insignia, looked quite amiable. He was tall and broad, with a pudgy face, round eyes,

and a slouching walk. There was, Jan thought, something vaguely familiar about him.

'Here, boy,' said the officer as Jan drew near. 'You
look strong. Can you clean floors?'

Jan was about to reply that he had never tried, when
he remembered that every skill was useful in Terezin.
So he dutifully replied, 'Yes, sir.'

'Good. You can clean my floors for me. The fellow who
used to do them has just died.'

As Jan followed the officer into one of the neat little
houses, his first reaction was anger. The rooms were
cosy, the furniture gleaming, and the bed so inviting,
with its snowy pillows and plump duvet, that Jan -
thinking of his own flea-ridden bunk - could hardly bear
to look at it. A pot of coffee was simmering in the kitchen,
and the smell of it nearly drove him mad.

'Here,' said his new master, presenting him with a
bucket, a scrubbing-brush and a bar of soap. 'There's
plenty of hot water in the tap. Just get on with it and
don't bother me.' And, so saying, he poured himself a
mug of coffee and went into the living-room, sank into an
armchair, and began to read a German newspaper.

At first Jan worked nervously, sloshing the soapy
water clumsily over the floors, but soon the officer fell
asleep with his newspaper over his face, and Jan grew
more confident. Now that he had wiped them dry, the
floors looked clean and bright and Jan felt proud of his
handiwork. Reassured by the sound of heavy snoring, he
roamed round the living-room, looking at the pictures
and ornaments and trying not to see the box of choco-
lates that lay enticingly open on the sideboard. Alongside the chocolate box was a large framed photograph in
which the Nazi officer posed smiling in a sunlit garden
with a woman in a flowery dress and two young boys.
One of them, Jan noticed, looked about his own age. He
wondered whether the boy knew, back home in Germany, what his father was doing to other children in

Czechoslovakia.

Suddenly the snoring stopped, and the officer woke and rubbed his eyes. At first he looked at Jan with a puzzled air; then he remembered, and asked, 'Why aren't you working?'

'Please sir, I've finished,' replied Jan.

The man heaved himself out of his armchair and began to inspect the floors, while Jan watched anxiously. Much to his relief, his new master smiled and patted his head.

'I'm glad that other fellow's dead,' he said amiably. '*You* do a much better job. Here, boy, here's something for you.' And, much to Jan's delight, the officer opened his kitchen larder and took out an enormous sticky bun thickly encrusted with sugar. Jan gazed at it in rapture, scarcely daring to dream that it was his.

'I'll wrap it for you,' said the officer kindly, 'or else some greedy young vulture will take it off you.' Then, as he put the treasure in a paper bag, he added, 'Can you polish boots?'

This time Jan did not hesitate, but answered, 'Yes, sir.'

'And cook scrambled eggs?'

'Y-yes, sir.'

'Good. You can come again tomorrow. What's your name?'

'Jan, sir.'

'How old are you?'

'Thir ... I mean fourteen.'

'I've got a boy of your age.'

Jan wanted to say, 'I know', but he thought better of it, bowed politely to his new employer, and ran back to his barracks, clutching the precious paper bag to his chest. He searched for Evald, and the two boys climbed eagerly into Jan's bunk. There, hidden from the prying eyes of the other children, they shared the bun, eating as slowly as they could and allowing the delicious sugar

86

crust to melt on their tongues.

'Mmm, it's full of raisins,' gulped Evald. 'I'll never forget this, Jan. This is the best day I've had since I came to Terezin.' And Jan, licking the sugar and cinnamon from his fingers, could not help but agree.

That night, lying in his bunk, his stomach feeling more comfortable than it had done for many a night, Jan suddenly remembered why it was that the German officer had seemed familiar.

'He looks like Yossel,' he thought. 'Yossel the Golem. He's got the same heavy, clumsy look. He even *walks* like Yossel. I wonder ... I wonder ...'

And Jan fell asleep wondering whether Rabbi Loewe had indeed sent the Golem to help him in his hour of need.

Next day Jan called on the Nazi officer again. This time he was given high leather boots and silver cutlery to polish, and a bar of chocolate by way of reward. After that it was understood that he was to be a regular visitor to the little house on the square.

His new employer, Jan learned, was called Hans Kolb (though Jan always thought of him as 'Yossel'), and he had been a baker in his home town of Hamburg. He treated Jan quite kindly, talking about life in Germany and his wife and children as the boy scrubbed and polished, swept and cooked. Jan found himself in possession of all kinds of talents that he had never dreamed of back in Prague. In particular, he was good at scrambling eggs. Sometimes Sergeant Kolb allowed him to eat a spoonful as he piled the creamy yellow mixture onto slices of crisp golden toast. And he often rewarded him - sometimes with a bun or chocolate, sometimes with a slice of cake, which Jan would take back to the barracks to share with Evald.

'It's not really fair ... *I've* never given *you* anything,' Evald said one day, as they huddled in Jan's bunk, lingering over a sumptuous slice of strudel.

'You're my friend,' said Jan, feeling embarrassed. 'That's more important than cake. Besides, *you* would share with *me* if you had anything, wouldn't you?'

Evald stopped chewing, and thought carefully.

'I don't know,' he replied at last.

'Do you mean you wouldn't ...?'

'Well, I used to share with my friends at school,' Evald added quickly, 'but that was easy. I wasn't hungry then. It's much harder to share in a place like this. Even fat Frantisek never gives anything away.'

Fat Frantisek, who was not really as fat as his name implied, was a specially favoured prisoner in Jan's barracks. He enjoyed special privileges because he was only half-Jewish, and because his non-Jewish grandfather was a distinguished general in Hitler's army. Everybody hated him, and he kept himself to himself. It was rumoured that he had extra blankets and a more comfortable mattress on his bunk, and he was often seen receiving food parcels, which he ate furtively under the blankets. All the children enjoyed insulting him, though nobody ever dared to hit him.

'There's one like him in every barracks,' said Evald gloomily. 'And they're all alike.'

'I feel rather sorry for Frantisek,' replied Jan. 'He hasn't any friends. If only he would learn to share ... '

Evald smiled.

'Oh, he shares all right,' he said, 'but he doesn't know anything about it.'

'What do you mean?'

Then Evald explained that Anna, not content with merely stealing food from the Nazi officers' kitchen, would often remove choice titbits from food parcels and pass them on to the other children, and that Frantisek was a frequent contributor.

'Just little things that he won't miss,' added Evald. 'The odd packet of biscuits or bar of chocolate.'

'Any sardines?' asked Jan, trying not to sound shocked.

'Up till now they've always run out before it got to my turn. That's just my luck. But Anna's promised me a sardine out of Fatso's next tin.'

'B-but that's stealing!' cried Jan, unable to contain his feelings any longer.

'And what's wrong with stealing?' retorted Evald angrily. 'We all steal. We all lie. We all cheat. We have to. Some of us even suck up to German officers.'

Then, as Jan blushed miserably, Evald added, 'There's no harm in it, not *here*. You'll learn, my friend. You'll soon learn.'

One morning, a woman came into Jan's barracks, and looked about her enquiringly. Jan already knew her by sight. Her name was Friedl Dicker-Brandejsova, and she had been a famous artist before the war. In Terezin she devoted herself to the children, giving them art lessons in an attempt to make their lives more bearable.

Seeing Jan watching her, she approached him. Her smile, he thought, seemed to light up the dark, gloomy room.

'Do you like drawing?' she asked, without bothering to introduce herself. 'Would you like to come to my art class?' Then, before he could stutter a reply, she went on, 'All my pupils are girls today. They always seem to outnumber the boys, but today I don't have a single boy, and I do like mixed classes. They're more fun, don't you think?' Her eyes twinkled, and Jan - though he had been hopeless at art in school - found himself, rather to his own surprise, agreeing to join her class.

'Can you bring some of your friends?' she went on, and Evald and two or three of the other boys were soon reluctantly trailing behind Jan as Friedl led them towards an adjoining barracks.

Here several little girls were eagerly awaiting their

art lesson. Their classroom, Jan noticed, was not like the art rooms he had known at school. There were no desks or easels, no paints or palettes, no art materials at all, in fact, apart from a few pencils and crayons and a great deal of wrapping-paper which had been saved, as Friedl later explained, from the parcels that came into the camp.

Jan was also shocked to learn that the art lessons, like those of the academic kind, were forbidden by the Nazis on pain of death, and that a look-out again had to be posted to give warning of unwelcome visitors. Watching the little girls happily wielding their crayons or making collage pictures with scraps of coloured paper, Jan wondered how the Nazis could possibly feel threatened by small children.

Paper and pencils were distributed to the new arrivals, and Jan and his friends joined in the art class - unwillingly at first, but with growing enthusiasm. Meanwhile Friedl moved quietly among her pupils, admiring their pictures and helping and encouraging the younger ones.

Jan, who had been accustomed to copying boring bowls of fruit or flowers in art classes at school, was rather shocked to find a macabre scene materializing on his brown paper. From his pencil emerged a shrivelled old woman clutching a begging bowl, a huddle of skinny children, and a cart loaded with coffins. Leaning across to look at Evald's picture, he saw a grisly gallows complete with a dangling corpse, and grimaced.

After a while, Friedl stopped the class and suggested that the young artists might like to see each others' pictures. As each drawing was held up for inspection, Jan was surprised to see that whereas all the boys had drawn gallows and coffins and gaunt prisoners, the girls' pictures were mainly sunny landscapes and gentle recollections of life gone by.

'Trust girls to draw happy pictures!' whispered Evald

to Jan as an older girl named Helga Pollekova produced a collage showing a farmer ploughing in a sunlit meadow.

'*Happy* pictures? In a place like this?' snorted a boy whose own picture showed an SS guard setting a dog on a wretched prisoner.

The next drawing, by a very small girl named Eva Winternitzova, showed a family seated at a meal. There were flowers on the table and pictures on the wall; the father wore a hat and the mother carried a handbag. There was something so sad and innocent about this picture that Jan felt his eyes smarting.

'Julie Ogularova?' said Friedl, and another little girl eagerly held up a drawing of a winter scene. A long procession of toboggans slid down a snowy hillside; a smiling snowman brandished a broom in the foreground, and in the background children played happily outside houses that had leafless trees in their gardens and smoke curling gently from their chimneys.

'That was my birthday, two years ago,' explained Julie. 'My Mummy and Daddy bought me a new sled, and we had a birthday tea. It was a lovely day.' Julie's lips trembled, and she pressed her knuckles against her eyes.

'It's a beautiful picture, Julie,' said Friedl. 'Children, have you noticed how the girls usually choose to remember the past while the boys prefer to confront the things we are enduring today?'

'Is that better, Miss?' asked one of the boys.

'Neither is better,' replied Friedl firmly. 'You must draw whatever gives you strength and comfort. As long as you draw. The drawing is the important thing.'

'If *you* want to draw happy things, why don't you draw a sardine?' whispered Jan to Evald, and was pleased to hear him giggle. 'Better still, why don't you draw a whole tinful?'

When the class was over, Friedl came over to Jan and thanked him, with a pleasant smile, for persuading his friends to come to her art class.

'I hope you'll come again,' she added. 'By the way, I don't even know your name.'

'My name's Jan Weiss,' replied Jan, and was surprised to see a look of recognition on Friedl's face.

'*I* know a Jan Weiss,' she said. 'At least, I know *of* him. My friend Marta Weiss's son is called Jan, but he's in hiding in Prague.'

Jan stared at Friedl, feeling as if he were dreaming.

'But *I'm* Marta's son,' he gasped, as soon as he could speak. 'I *was* in hiding, but I'm here now. Did you say my mother was your friend? Is she here now? How is she? Oh, *please* tell me ...'

Then he saw Friedl was looking sad, and his voice dwindled into silence.

'Jan, you must be brave,' she said at last.

'Is she dead?'

'No, but she's very ill. She's in the hospital. I'll take you there. She's got typhus, Jan. She's dying.'

9

It was, Jan thought, quite unlike any hospital he had ever seen. The place was bare and uncurtained and totally without comfort. There were no beds.The patients lay packed together, row upon row, on heaps of straw or blankets spread on the floor. They tossed uneasily, groaned occasionally, or slept.

At first he did not recognize the woman who lay at his feet. She was gaunt, grey-haired and dressed in a ragged shirt, with the face of a stranger. He knew it was his mother only because Friedl had stopped, and was bending over her.

'Marta,' she said in a low voice, and the woman opened her eyes.

'My head aches,' she whispered.

'I know, dear,' replied Friedl. 'There's nothing I can do. There's no more medicine, the doctor says. But I've got something better for you than medicine.' And she pushed Jan forward so that the sick woman could see him.

For a few moments, his mother stared at him. Then an expression of recognition and joy came over her face, to be followed at once by a look of alarm.

'Jan!' she cried. 'Oh Jan, my darling, what are you doing here? *Why* are you here? You should be safe in Prague!' Two bony hands reached out to clasp his, and Jan shivered.

'They were arrested,' he stammered. 'They ... the Nemecs ... they were taken away. And I came here because I wanted to find you ...' He broke off, and found himself hugging his mother tightly, shocked to feel how thin and fragile she had become.

'You mustn't ...' she gasped, pushing him away. 'You shouldn't be here. I've got typhus. I don't want you to catch it.'

'Oh, I shan't catch it,' replied Jan, trying to laugh. 'Don't you remember, Mother, I never did catch anything? Not even when we had exams coming up, and I wanted to get off school?'

Mother smiled.

'I remember,' she said. 'It was always Pavlina who caught whatever was going.'

'Mother, where *is* Pavlina?' asked Jan eagerly. 'And Monika, and Grandpa? I've been looking for them ever since I came here. I've been asking, but no one seems to know.'

Before Mother could answer, Friedl quietly said, 'I'll leave you alone together, shall I?' Then she moved away and began to talk to a woman who held a thermometer and whom Jan took to be a nurse, although she wore a shabby dress instead of the crisply-starched uniform he had always associated with hospitals.

Mother's eyes had closed again, and Jan pressed her hand gently.

'Pavlina and Monika?' he asked again.

Her eyes opened, and she looked at him mournfully.

'They were taken away,' she said. 'Grandpa too.'

'When?'

'On the very first day.'

'Where were they taken?'

'Somewhere in the East. A place called Auschwitz-Birkenau. Some people told me it was a work-camp. Others said it was a place where they could rest. I don't

94

think it *could* have been a work-camp. Most of the people who went there were children and old people.'

'Then it must be a rest camp,' said Jan consolingly. 'Have you heard from them?'

'Not since the first postcard,' replied Mother. 'I had a card from Grandpa, saying they were happy and settling in well. But I've heard nothing since, and I'm getting worried. Perhaps Grandpa isn't alive any more.'

Before Jan could say something reassuring, she gripped his hand fiercely.

'But the girls are alive,' she cried. 'They're young and strong, and they've all their lives before them. *I* shall never see them again, but you must find them, Jan.'

'I ... I ...'

'I wish you could have seen them, when the Germans took them away,' Mother went on, her eyes glittering. 'I didn't recognize my little girls ... they were so brave. Do you remember how they used to squabble? I used to worry that we had spoiled them too much. But they grew up on that day. Pavlina looked after Monika like a little mother. I was so proud of them! Jan, promise me that you'll go after them and find them. I want you to be a family again.'

'I promise,' said Jan, and his mother sighed gently, and closed her eyes.

'Have you heard anything from Father?' Jan began after a pause. Then he became aware that Friedl and the nurse were standing beside him. The nurse bent down to wipe the sweat from Mother's face. She felt for her pulse and then straightened herself, and looked at Jan sadly.

'She's gone,' she said. 'I'm so sorry.'

Friedl put a consoling arm about him, but Jan for some reason felt quite calm. The gaunt, shrivelled woman lying on the floor was not his mother, he told himself. *His* mother was still the pretty young woman who had once laughed and poured coffee and presided over lavish birthday parties in the house in Krizovnicka Street.

Mother's ashes were thrown in the little river, and life in Terezin went on much as usual, except that Jan had a new purpose. He now *wanted* to be transported East, and waited eagerly for his name to be called. Somewhere in that unknown land Pavlina and Monika, and perhaps Grandpa too, were waiting for him. He would keep his promise to Mother, and find them again.

He kept his eyes wide open now, and saw that other children in his barracks were regularly rounded up for the transports. And he noticed that these children were almost invariably orphans, the most sick and emaciated ones, the ones without friends or hope. Children like Frantisek, who received food parcels, never found their names on the transport lists.

'Which proves that the East can't be anywhere very pleasant,' said Evald. 'If it was, you can bet fat Frantisek would be on the train.'

A few days after this conversation, it was Evald's turn to be called up for transport. His name was posted on the notice-board, and he was issued with a number and told to report to the large courtyard of the Hamburg Barracks. As Jan sat unhappily watching him packing his belongings, such as they were, into a bag, he saw that his friend's thin hands were trembling.

'I knew it had to happen one day,' Evald admitted, 'but I'm scared.'

'I wish I could go with you,' said Jan truthfully. 'Or go instead of you.'

'You must be crazy ...' Evald began.

'No, I mean it. My sisters are there,' replied Jan. 'Perhaps you could look out for them.'

'What do they look like?'

'Oh, you know, little kids ... I expect they've grown

since I last saw them. If you *do* come across them, write and tell me, won't you?'

When Jan saw Ivo that evening, he asked if he was allowed to volunteer for the transport, explaining that his family had been sent East and he wanted to find them. To his surprise, Ivo laughed and clapped him on the back.

'Don't be so bold, my young hero,' he said. 'Wait your turn for the transport. It will come soon enough.'

Jan had little opportunity to puzzle over Ivo's remark, for most of his time was now spent trying to keep up Evald's spirits. When the morning of the transport came, he was allowed to accompany his friend to the Hamburg Barracks adjoining the railway station, where the prisoners chosen for the transport were assembling. There were several hundred of them, all clutching their bags or suitcases and wearing numbers round their necks. In the courtyard a small orchestra was playing a lively polka. Beyond the gates of the Barracks the platform waited, and beyond that the train, its engine belching heavy smoke.

Relatives and friends had come to say good-bye to most of the prisoners, and Jan saw Anna bidding a tearful farewell to her friends Blanche and Magda, who were going on the transport. They hugged and kissed each other, and Anna gave each a slice of cake for the journey and presented Blanche with a home-made pincushion made from a scrap of green velvet, and Magda with a calendar. 'It's out of date,' Jan heard her say, 'but the pictures are pretty. It's just to remember me by.'

'I'm sorry I haven't got a pincushion for *you*, or anything pretty,' said Jan, desperately trying to make Evald smile. 'But I've got something to eat on the journey, or else when you get there. Look.' And he drew out of his pocket a large bar of nut chocolate, which he waved before Evald's eyes. 'Sergeant Kolb gave it to me for cleaning his lavatory, and I kept it hidden in my mattress all night. You're jolly lucky that I didn't eat it.'

'Thank you, Jan, you've always been decent to me,' said Evald humbly. 'I've never given *you* anything.'

'That's all right. I'm sorry it's not a tin of sardines,' replied Jan. He felt a sudden urge to hug Evald, and wondered whether Evald would be embarrassed. Then he noticed that other people seemed to be embracing, and he nervously pressed his arms round Evald's thin shoulders. Rather to his surprise, Evald did not edge away. All he said was, 'I'll miss you.'

'And me you. Don't forget to write.'

Jan was aware that the prisoners were now beginning to surge towards the platform gates, helped on their way by Nazi officers with whips and truncheons. He did not say good-bye to Evald, but watched and waved till he was swallowed up in the crowd. Then he turned away, not wanting to see the train set out on its mysterious journey.

That night Jan slept uneasily, knowing that Evald was no longer in the adjoining bunk. Next day he noticed that several other children were missing from his room and that nearly everyone seemed to be mourning the loss of a friend.

'If only we knew *where* they've gone,' said Josef sadly.

'It's better not to know,' said Hanus. 'My parents got a postcard from my uncle. It was very mysterious ...'

'How, mysterious?' asked Jan.

'Well, it was just an ordinary postcard, from a place called Auschwitz-Birkenau. He said he was happy, and settling in well. But on the edge of the card he'd written two words in Hebrew, so that the Germans wouldn't understand. One of the words meant "death" and the other meant "gas" ...'

'Gas?' echoed Jan, puzzled. 'Why gas?'

'That's peculiar,' interrupted Josef. 'Do you remember those children from Bialystok?'

How could they not remember? thought Jan. It had been a very strange episode. Fifteen hundred children, dressed in rags and thin as scarecrows, had arrived in Terezin on a special transport. The residents of the ghetto had all been locked in their houses as the children were marched through the streets, and had been forbidden on pain of death to talk to them. But rumours had filtered through. The prisoners who had washed and deloused them later told how the children, on seeing the signs on the showers and delousing station, had screamed 'Gas! Gas!' and had refused to enter the building. It was whispered that they had seen terrible things ... that they had seen their parents killed ... After a few weeks, the Bialystok children had been removed on another transport, and were never seen again.

'Why did they scream "gas"?' asked Josef.

'I once had some teeth out by gas,' said Jan. 'It was horrible. I nearly died.'

'Does it mean they pull your teeth out when you get there?' asked one of the smaller children in alarm.

'No, I shouldn't think it's anything to do with teeth,' said Hanus. 'But my parents never heard from my uncle again.'

The promised postcard from Evald arrived a few weeks later, when Jan had almost given up hope. Evald wrote that he was in Auschwitz-Birkenau, and was well and happy. He made no mention of Pavlina or Monika. Jan carefully examined the postcard from all angles, but could see no Hebrew words, or any secret references to 'death' or 'gas'.

He never heard from Evald again.

10

At first, Jan missed Evald dreadfully, but after a while he found another 'best friend'. This was a boy named Pavel Friedman, who was younger than Jan but seemed older than his years.

Summer and autumn now gave way to a long dragging winter, and the suffering increased. Fleabites turned to frostbite; chilblains made Jan's toes swell and itch inside his cracked boots; rats swarmed into the barracks for shelter. There was no heating, and neither the prisoners' shabby clothes nor their worn bedclothes kept out the bitter cold. Queuing for meals, and for the wash-basins and lavatories, became a greater ordeal than ever, and the water froze in the taps. Worse still, though the cold weather increased the prisoners' appetites, no extra food was provided, and Jan sometimes felt he was dying of hunger. He knew that the other children stole food, and would have done so himself had he not been afraid that either God or the Nazis would punish him. In the fields the spades and hoes of the working-parties could scarcely penetrate the frozen earth. Luckily, deep snow soon covered the ground and made further digging impossible. Jan, thanks to Ivo, was given a new job in a metal workshop, where he could at least stay indoors out of the snow and rain.

One dark, dank day in November, a census was taken to determine how many Jewish prisoners the camp contained. Some forty-seven thousand people were massed in the main square and forced to stand all day in the rain without food or drink. After several hours the crowds panicked; many people collapsed, and many more were trampled to death. It was later learned that three hundred people had died.

Eventually the long winter passed; the wind grew less keen, and green leaves and blossom at last began to break from the bare trees around the camp. Jan saw crocuses glimmering in the little gardens on the square, and rejoiced that he had lived through the cruellest time of the year.

To his surprise, he realized that he had grown taller despite the lack of food. Although his clothes hung on his thin body, his sleeves and trouser-legs were now too short for his lengthening arms and legs, and new clothes had to be found for him by the children's department. These were not exactly new; they were cast-offs left behind by a boy who had been transported East, and were as worn and patched as his own clothes had been. But at least they fitted him, and after they had passed through the laundry they looked almost presentable.

Meanwhile he continued to work for Sergeant Kolb, scrubbing his floors, cleaning boots and even cooking his meals. In return he occasionally received buns and chocolate bars and slabs of cake or fine white bread. But better even than the food was the feeling that he had found a protector. Sergeant Kolb, who still reminded Jan of Yossel the Golem, talked to him about his family and his baker's shop in Hamburg and stood up for him against the jibes of his fellow-officers. When his next-door neighbour, Sergeant Putsch, kicked Jan and called him 'Jewboy', Sergeant Kolb went so far as to say, 'Leave him alone, Ernst ... he's worth ten of you.' However bad life was, thought Jan, it could still have been worse.

As April approached, Jan realized that secret preparations were being made for the celebration of Passover, the Jewish festival that commemorated the liberation of the Ancient Israelites from Egypt. Although special

Passover food could not be provided, flour was somehow smuggled into the bakery to produce some matzos, the cakes of unleavened bread that were required for the Seder, the ceremony that symbolized the Exodus.

Jan's own barracks had its own Seder, led by one of the many Rabbis who were prisoners in Terezin. Huddled around the makeshift table with the other children, Jan remembered the Seder at home in Krizovnicka Street, the candles and wine and silver goblets, the cushioned chairs, the matzos under their gold-embroidered cloth, and the festive meal that came between the prayers and the songs. But the theme, that of deliverance from slavery, was more powerful now than it had ever been, though this year's ceremony was conducted in an undertone so that the Nazi guards might not hear. The youngest boy asked why this night was different from all other nights. Then the hungry children listened intently as the Rabbi, an old man with a white beard, replied, 'In every generation men rise against us, but the Holy One, blessed be He, delivers us from their hand ... Let all who are hungry come and eat; may all who are needy come and feast with us ... This year we are slaves; next year we shall be free men.'

Later that spring, Jan suddenly became aware that strange things were happening in Terezin. Some time earlier, the street numbers and letters had been replaced by names such as Park Street, Town Hall Square and Riverside Road, which sounded much friendlier and gave the camp the atmosphere of a real town. Now, much to the surprise of the prisoners, builders and decorators arrived and began to replace broken windows and brighten up the derelict buildings with pastel-coloured paint. Next came new furniture, chintzy curtains and lampshades, comfortable blankets, duvets, and even window-boxes filled with flowers.

More incredibly still, workmen arrived to put up

brand-new buildings and by that summer Terezin could boast a splendid dining-hall and communal centre, a sports centre with football pitch, dressing-rooms and showers, a bandstand and - best of all - a glass-covered children's pavilion complete with a slide, swings and a paddling-pool. Green turf was laid down throughout the ghetto, and newly-planted flower gardens were a blaze of colour. A more macabre note was provided by a mock cemetery with imitation graves and a 'memorial' to the thousands of Jews who had died in the camp.

At first the children could not believe their eyes. But any suggestion that the Nazis might have undergone a change of heart was soon dispelled by Ivo, who had learned the truth from a member of the Jewish Council and passed it on to his young charges. 'Don't believe all you see,' he said bitterly. 'A delegation from the International Red Cross is due to visit Terezin next month to see just how Hitler is treating his Jews, and the Commandant is determined that they'll go away satisfied. They'll take the Nazis' lies back to the free world, and then everyone will forget us again. Enjoy yourselves while it lasts, children. It won't last long, believe me.'

Being invited to enjoy themselves, the children needed no second bidding. Wide-eyed and fascinated, they watched Terezin blossoming into the model town it had always pretended to be. Special events were carefully rehearsed for the day of the visit, from a football match and a children's party to plays, mimes, a wonderful concert version of Verdi's *Requiem* and a children's opera called *Brundibar* in which Jan, who had a good singing voice, took part with gusto. On the eve of June 23rd, the day of the Red Cross visit, roses specially flown in from Holland were planted in the town square, and fresh fruit, vegetables and other tempting foodstuffs were brought in to stock the empty shops.

It was rumoured that Adolf Eichmann, who had special charge of Terezin, together with other high-ranking Nazi officials, would attend the performance of Verdi's *Requiem*. A hospital was transformed for the occasion into a concert hall. Jan later heard that the sick people in the hospital had been cleared out to make room for the concert, and sent to Auschwitz-Birkenau.

June 23rd dawned bright and sunny, and for the first time in over a year Jan emerged from his bunk feeling eager to face the day. An air of excitement hung over the ghetto; it was almost as if the children, at least, believed in the great lie they were being forced to perpetrate.

The delegates from the Red Cross arrived on time, and walked through the ghetto smiling benevolently as they saw all the improvements that had been introduced for their benefit. The Commandant and some of his senior officers accompanied the guests, all wearing kindly, unfamiliar smiles. Jan grimaced when he saw the usually ferocious Commandant stop to pat little Jewish children on the head, and heard them call him 'uncle' as they had been instructed.

Pavel was so incensed that he nearly choked. 'Do you think our honoured guests are really fooled?' he muttered. 'How would it be if I were to tell them the truth?' And Jan, alarmed now, begged him to keep quiet.

Meanwhile, everything went strictly according to plan. A group of girls marched singing to their work in the fields, hoes and rakes balanced jauntily on their shoulders. Newly-baked loaves were unloaded in front of the baker's shop, and the café for once provided real coffee and delicious cakes. The Red Cross delegation visited the invalids in the sick-rooms and the children in their classrooms, where the normally forbidden lessons were in progress, and they reached the football pitch just in time to see a goal being scored. In the concert hall, the delegates sat with the pale, owlishly bespectacled Adolph Eichmann and other important Nazis and heard the prisoners' voices uplifted triumphantly in Verdi's music. At midday they were taken to the mess-hall where, served by smiling waitresses in starched aprons, they ate a tasty meal with brand-new cutlery off snowy-white tablecloths. The prisoners, the Commandant assured them, always ate exactly the same food.

For the children, especially, the day was one to remember. They played on the slides and swings, performed their own opera, and - best of all - were feasted at a long table laden with delicacies. They had been told to call out, 'We're tired of sardines, uncle!' as the ever-smiling Commandant walked past with the Red Cross gentlemen. Jan, looking at the oily little fish that nestled on their plates, thought sadly of Evald, and wondered again what had become of him.

Sadly, the children's party came to an end as soon as the delegates had passed, and all the delicious food was abruptly removed. One little boy, who was crying because a pink-iced cake had been snatched away from him before he could finish eating it, was consoled by Friedl Dicker-Brandejsova, who had volunteered to act as a helper at the party.

'I know,' she said cheerfully. 'Why don't you *draw* a pink-iced cake when you get back to your room? Then you'll be able to keep it.'

The little boy blinked away his tears, considered the idea carefully, and then smiled.

'I will,' he replied. 'I'll draw *two* cakes. And I'll draw myself eating both of them.'

The Red Cross delegates left Terezin that night, and the prisoners expected dismantling of the ghetto's 'new look' to begin next day. Much to their surprise, the cushions and lampshades remained in place, and so did the flower-gardens, the concert-hall, the children's pavilion, and all the other improvements. Jan prayed that it was all going to last, and was disappointed when Ivo finally explained what was happening. It seemed that the Commandant was planning to make a film, to be called *Terezin Spa*, which would allow cinema audiences in the outside world to see just how well the Jews were being treated under Nazi rule. 'It's crazy,' Ivo repeated, 'but it's a blessing while it lasts. So let's make the most of it, shall we, boys?'

Filming took place in August, under the direction of Kurt Gerron, a famous German film director who was a prisoner in the camp. The same charade that had been acted before the Red Cross delegates was now played out before the cameras. The Nazi officials wore kindly smiles once again; girls sang on their way to work; the music of Verdi's *Requiem* filled the summer air, and the children feasted on sardines and iced cakes and called the Commandant 'uncle'.

But of course it could not last for ever. The day came when the last camera was wound down; the last arc-lamp switched off, and the last reel of film placed in its canister. The Commandant stopped smiling; the food and flowers, cushions and curtains were taken away and the new buildings pulled down. Terezin reverted to its old, grey, sad and hungry self. Only the music remained to remind the Jews of those few incredible weeks, and even this did not last long. As soon as filming was over, Kurt Gerron and his assistants, the choir that had performed Verdi's *Requiem*, and its director Raphael Schächter, were rounded up and transported East.

August was now drawing to its close. The days were growing shorter, and in the German officers' gardens brilliant summer blossoms were giving way to the deeper bronze and gold and crimson flowers of Autumn. Jan was walking one day with Pavel when a butterfly fluttered over the rooftops, hovered for a few moments, and then vanished into the deep blue sky.

'That's strange,' said Pavel. 'I thought *mine* was the last butterfly, but now we've seen another.'

'What do you mean?' asked Jan, puzzled.

'I wrote a poem about a butterfly once,' replied Pavel. 'It was soon after I arrived here. I thought I would never see another. My poem was published in the camp magazine.'

'*Published?*' said Jan, much impressed. 'I'd like to hear it. Do you remember the words?'

'I ... I can't remember.'

'Yes you can. Go on, tell me what you wrote.'

So Pavel recited his poem, while the two boys walked past rotting heaps of garbage and watched a laden coffin-cart trundling along the street.

> 'The last, the very last,' said Pavel,
> 'So richly, brightly, dazzlingly yellow,
> Perhaps if the sun's tears would sing
> against a white stone ...
>
> Such, such a yellow
> Is carried lightly way up high.
> It went away, I'm sure, because it wished
> to kiss the world good-bye.
> For seven weeks I've lived in here,
> Penned up inside this ghetto,
> But I have found my people here.
> The dandelions call to me,
> And the white chestnut candles in the court.
> Only I never saw another butterfly.
>
> That butterfly was the last one.
> Butterflies don't live in here,
> in the ghetto.'

'That's beautiful,' said Jan. 'You're very clever.' For some reason he felt sad that Pavel was clever, and that his poem was so good, though he could not quite understand why.

'I got it wrong,' said Pavel, laughing. 'The butterfly in my poem *wasn't* the last one. But this one will be.'

'How do you know?'

'If *you* were a butterfly, would *you* want to stay here? You'll see, we won't see another one.'

Pavel was right. In the short time that he and Jan had left in Terezin, they never saw another butterfly.

11

A few days later, Anna came into Jan's room looking excited.

'I don't know if any of you know,' she announced, 'but old Mrs Kadarova is having her ninetieth birthday next week.'

'Who's Mrs Kadarova?' asked Pavel.

'A sweet old lady,' replied Anna. 'She lives in an awful little room with some other old ladies. They don't even have any bunks. They all sleep on the floor. And she's lost all her family. Just imagine celebrating your ninetieth birthday in a place like this!'

The boys agreed that it was not a cheerful prospect.

'So I thought it would be nice,' Anna went on, 'if some of us could give her a party.'

The boys stared at her, convinced that she had gone mad. Then Pavel spoke the words that were in all their minds.

'What are we going to do for food?' he asked.

'Oh, I've thought about that,' replied Anna airily. 'There won't be much, of course. I'll borrow as much as I can from the officers' kitchen. And we could all save up our sugar and margarine rations, and I could get Ivana to make a birthday cake. And we could save our bread and jam rations. And there might be some food parcels. Anyway, it's not going to be a food party.'

'Food parties are best,' said Jan, and the other boys applauded. But Anna was undaunted.

'I've got lots of girls to help me organize this party,' she went on, 'but I need a few boys. All-girls' parties are so boring, don't you think?'

'We're not going to play kissing games, are we?' asked a small boy in alarm, and everyone laughed.

'Not if you don't want to,' replied Anna cheerfully. 'Besides, I only need a few of you. We'll have games, of course, and we can have songs and dances, and recitations, and perhaps Friedl can make us some paper hats. Some of the girls are going to put on a play. And we can make Mrs Kadarova some birthday cards. Nice cheerful cards, please, not pictures of people being hanged. And I thought we might organize a few presents. *I've* got a nearly-new hair-ribbon I could give her.'

'I still think food is best,' said Jan.

'So do I,' sighed Anna. 'I'll do what I can.'

At this moment Frantisek, who as usual was being ignored by the other boys, spoke up unexpectedly.

'I ... I had a food parcel today,' he said nervously. 'I ... I've eaten some of it, but there's still some biscuits and sweets left. And a bag of raisins. You can have those, if you like.'

For a few moments the other boys stared at him in astonishment. Then someone piped up, 'Good old Frantisek!' and the fat boy flushed with pleasure.

During the next few days, Jan found himself looking forward to Mrs Kadarova's party with something that was almost excitement.

He knew, of course, that it would be nothing like the parties of his school-days, with their jellies and trifles and the iced birthday cakes ablaze with candles. It would not even be anything like Grandpa's seventieth birthday party, which had been a more adult affair, with lots of smoked salmon and champagne and cigars. But it seemed a good thing to bring some happiness to an old lady who had no family. Besides, he liked the idea of the children having a real party of their own, not a fake party set up by the Nazis to deceive the outside world.

So he persuaded Pavel to recite his butterfly poem while he himself rehearsed a German folk song that had been one of Grandpa's favourites. And in Friedl's art class the children who were organizing the party made birthday cards for Mrs Kadarova, the boys forcing themselves to draw flowers, birds and pretty landscapes instead of the ghastly scenes that came to them more readily.

Meanwhile, Anna occupied herself with stealing food from the Nazi kitchens and supervising the baking of a birthday cake in the children's cookhouse. It was a sponge cake, she announced proudly, made with real eggs and sandwiched with real apricot jam. Everyone who came to the party would receive a slice. Jan found the cake appearing in his nightly dreams.

Jan's work schedule in the fields finished at midday, and on the day of the party he hurried home to the barracks as quickly as he could and took particular care with washing his hands and face. His clothes had recently come back from the laundry, and he had polished his boots with a damp rag, though without any polish. Better still, Sergeant Kolb had given him a bar of chocolate the previous day as a reward for cleaning his floors, and Jan had decided - with some reluctance - to give it to the old lady as a birthday present. The chocolate, together with his home-made birthday card, was now reposing securely under the blanket of his bunk, safe from prying eyes.

'I hope it won't melt,' he said to Pavel. 'The chocolate, I mean, not the card.'

'I wish *I* had a present for her,' replied Pavel sadly. 'I made a card, but it doesn't seem enough.'

'You can share *my* present,' said Jan cheerfully. 'After all, it *is* half yours, really. If I'd kept it, you would have had half, wouldn't you?'

'I wish *I* could get a job,' Pavel replied. 'But I'm not old enough.'

The afternoon, as usual, was taken up with lessons, after which the children were free to do as they pleased. At about four o'clock, Anna arrived at Jan's room to escort the party guests to old Mrs Kadarova's residence. Only eight boys had volunteered, but Anna assured the others that it did not matter. 'I've lots of girls,' she said cheerfully, 'and there are a dozen old ladies living in Mrs Kadarova's room, so there'll be about forty of us.'

To Jan, this was not good news. He found himself wondering dolefully if the birthday cake would be big enough to share out among forty ravenous guests.

Old Mrs Kadarova lived in a musty little room leading off a narrow, stinking alley. Ivo had told Jan that the old people received the worst treatment in Terezin, and Jan now saw for himself that this was true. The tiny windows admitted only a glimmer of daylight; the walls were grimy, and there was no furniture of any kind. In place of a table, the blankets on which the old ladies normally slept had been spread over the floor to form a cloth, and on this the meagre party food had been carefully laid out on makeshift paper plates. Apart from the bread and jam saved from the children's rations, there were delicacies which Anna had stolen from the SS kitchens, including some currant buns, carefully divided into forty more or less equal pieces, and two bottles of lemonade which would allow the guests a sip each. Each guest was likewise allotted a half-biscuit and three raisins from Frantisek's food parcel, as well as a single lick of one of the sweets. The old ladies were allowed a whole biscuit and a sweet each, while the birthday girl had two biscuits and two sweets all to herself. In the middle of the tablecloth was the birthday cake, a plain sponge decorated by Ivana, the children's cook, with coloured sugar in the form of a figure 90. Nine matches stuck round the rim of the cake took the place of birthday candles. Jan did not know whether to laugh or cry.

And yet old Mrs Kadarova, a tiny wrinkled woman who reminded Jan of a sparrow, seemed overjoyed as she hugged Anna and greeted the rest of the children, smiling with delight as they handed her their cards and presents. The other old ladies seemed equally excited. They were all, Jan noticed, wearing what seemed to be their best clothes, and Mrs Kadarova had a flower clip tucked into her piled-up hair. Anna saw it, and suddenly clasped her hands together in dismay.

'Oh, I forgot!' she exclaimed.

'What did you forget, lovey?' asked Mrs Kadarova.

'Flowers. I forgot to bring you any flowers. How stupid of me! How can you have a 90th birthday party without flowers?'

'I don't need any flowers, dear ... I've got everything I need already ...'

But Anna insisted that Mrs Kadarova must have flowers. She would get some instantly from the gardens of the SS billets. Just one or two roses from each garden, she said. Nobody would even notice that they were missing.

And before the old lady could protest any further, Anna was gone, running like the wind, her heavy dark plait swinging behind her. Mrs Kadarova laughed and shook her head.

'Ah, if everyone was like our Anna, Terezin would be a better place,' she said. 'She's a wonderful girl. I only had to mention that I was going to be ninety today, and she insisted that I must have this party. I pray God will keep her safe and reward her with a good husband ...'

Just then Friedl arrived with some party hats she had made for the old ladies out of scraps of coloured paper. She was pinning these to their scanty hair and apologizing for not having been able to make hats for the children as well, when Anna arrived back, flushed and

113

joyful. In one hand she carried a bucket of water, and in the other a bunch of flowers - not just roses, but also petunias and marigolds and large silvery-white daisies. Their brilliant colour and perfume seemed to fill the dingy room with sunlight, and Mrs Kadarova clapped her hands in delight.

'There were so many to choose from,' Anna explained, as she arranged the flowers in the bucket and then placed it on the tablecloth next to the birthday cake. 'Why shouldn't *they* spare us these? After all, they have so much, and we have so little.'

'Didn't anyone see you?' asked one of the old ladies anxiously.

'Not they. I hid the flowers under my shirt.'

'When are we going to eat?' asked a little boy, eyeing the flowers without much enthusiasm.

'Soon, soon. After we've had the entertainments.'

'Can't we eat first? I'm starving.'

Before Anna could reply, the other children joined in, all insisting so vehemently that they would be able to act, sing, dance and recite better *after* they had eaten that she was forced to give way. Soon the guests were all squatting on the floor round the cloth, their eyes fixed eagerly on the food, waiting for the signal to begin.

'Before we start,' said Mrs Kadarova, 'I should like to recite a Hebrew blessing I'm sure you all know. *I* never thought ever to hear it again.' And to Jan's surprise, she began to speak the blessing with which his father had always inaugurated the Jewish festivals in the old days. 'Blessed art thou, O Lord our God, King of the Universe,' quavered Mrs Kadarova, 'who hast kept us in life, and hast preserved us, and enabled us to reach this season.'

After that there was a long silence. All eyes were fixed on Anna. Then she smiled.

'All right,' she said. 'You can start now.'

The children needed no second invitation. Within a few moments the bread and jam and fragments of bun and biscuit had been ravenously eaten and the lemonade drunk and the tell-tale bottles hidden, and the sweets were being passed round so that each guest could enjoy a long, luxurious lick.

'It's not fair,' cried one little girl. 'The boys are sucking the sweets, not licking them.'

'Now boys, no cheating,' said Anna sternly. 'Only one lick each, or there won't be enough to go round.' Then, hearing murmurs of discontent from the boys, she quickly added, 'I think Mrs Kadarova ought to cut her birthday cake now.'

The angry murmurs subsided, and someone handed Mrs Kadarova a knife.

'We must light the candles first,' said Anna, taking a box of matches from her pocket. The guests watched, fascinated, as she ignited the nine matches round the edge of the cake so that the sugar 90 seemed to glow in a ring of tiny flames. Smiling, Mrs Kadarova inclined her small head, which was now encased in a green paper crown, and blew them out. The children clapped and sang 'Happy birthday', and somebody called out, 'Speech, speech!'

'Ladies and gentlemen,' began Mrs Kadarova. 'This is the nicest party I've ever had ...'

At that moment there came a thunderous knocking at the door.

It was the Commandant himself who stood in the open doorway, flanked by two grim henchmen. His eyes roamed round the room, and then came to rest on the flowers.

It seemed to Jan that everyone had stopped breathing. Then, after a few moments, the Commandant spoke.

'Aha, a party, I see,' he said.

Trembling, Mrs Kadarova raised her hand.

'If you please, Herr Commandant,' she said, 'today is

my ninetieth birthday, and some of the children were good enough to give me this little celebration ...'

'A ninetieth birthday party?' interrupted the Commandant with a smile. 'How touching. We don't have many of those. Why didn't you invite me?'

Jan felt himself relaxing. Was it possible, he thought, that the Commandant was going to be kind, just as he had been during the Red Cross visit? But the Commandant's next words shattered Jan's hopes.

'I recognize my prize petunias,' he said, and his face and voice were stern now. 'Am I to understand that they picked themselves and walked here?'

There was a long silence. Then the Commandant strode into the middle of the room, and brought his stick down on the shoulders of the nearest boy.

'I'm waiting for someone to own up!' he shouted. 'If no one admits to stealing these flowers, you'll all be severely punished. You all *deserve* to be punished, anyway. Where did this cake come from?'

'The children saved up their rations and baked it,' said Mrs Kadarova bravely.

'They stole the ingredients, more likely! However, I'm inclined to be lenient. If the thief who took my flowers owns up, I'll let the rest of you off.'

The room was as silent as if all its inhabitants were carved in stone. Jan felt his heart hammering. Then Anna suddenly jumped to her feet.

'It was me,' she cried. 'I took the flowers. And the party was my idea.'

A little moan came from the old ladies. Jan, to his own shame, felt himself sighing with relief. Then the Commandant smiled again.

'You've put me to a lot of trouble, young lady,' he said. 'I've had to knock on a great many doors to find you. I must tell you that we've had our eye on you for a long time. A lot of food seems to vanish from the kitchens where you work. I'm glad we've caught you red-handed at last. You won't be doing any more thieving.'

Some of the little girls began to cry, but Anna merely stared ahead defiantly as if she were not in the least frightened. The Commandant made a sign to his guards, and they seized Anna, tied her hands behind her back, and then frog-marched her out of the room. The Commandant picked up the flowers, and followed.

When the door had closed after them, pandemonium broke out. The old ladies and most of the girls were in tears, while the boys marvelled at how brave Anna had been. On the makeshift cloth the cake still stood uncut, its matches blackened and dead. They would never get to eat it now, Jan thought.

'That lovely young girl,' sobbed Mrs Kadarova. 'She's going to die for my sake!'

Jan felt his spine freeze. Surely, he thought, they were not going to do *that* to Anna, just for a few flowers!

Next day the children learned that Anna had been hanged in the Small Fortress.

The news of Anna's death filled Jan with terror. Until that time he had consoled himself with the thought that the Nazis, however bad they might be, would not kill children. But now that Anna, who was not much older than himself, had been put to death for such a small misdemeanour, Jan knew that no one was safe. Above all, he told himself, he must get out of this dreadful place. When he crawled into his bunk in the darkness that night, he fumbled about in the slit in his mattress, searching in the straw for his precious amulet. Then his fingers closed on the tiny golden bird, and he sighed with relief.

This time he knew exactly what he had to do. As he stroked the bird's head, he whispered again and again, 'Take me back to Rabbi Loewe's time! Take me back to his house.' There was an empty feeling in the pit of his stomach, a fear that the magic might not work any more.

But it did work. The familiar dizziness enveloped him, and when it subsided he was in the open air, standing in the cobbled alley between the tall, gaunt houses of medieval Prague.

Before him rose the heavy arched door of Rabbi Loewe's house. Jan drew a deep breath, and then hammered on the door with all his might. For some moments there was no reply. Then the door slowly opened, and Jan saw Jiri's face, its mouth open in surprise.

Behind him, a candle in her hand, stood Pearl, the Rebbetzin, and Jan ran into her arms with a glad cry.

12

Now that Jan was back in the Rabbi's house, he was amazed by its comfort and luxury. During his first visit he had found sixteenth-century Prague a cheerless, dark and inconvenient place compared with the Prague in which *he* had grown up. Now he discovered everything about it to be delightful, from the blazing log fires to the goose-feather pillows and the steaming broth, roast goose and quince pie. He felt he would never be able to stop eating. Best of all, he found himself once again being cossetted and cherished, as he had been by his parents before Hitler came to Prague.

There was something else, too, that gave him both pleasure and pain. He had become aware of it almost as soon as he returned to Rabbi Loewe's house. Suddenly he realized that he had put on flesh and muscle together with his sixteenth-century tunic and breeches; that his chest and shoulders felt broad and his legs firm, and that the arms he had flung around the Rebbetzin were brown and strong and unmarked by scabs and sores.

Pearl's eyes lit up as she looked at him.

'Yankel,' she cried. 'How big and beautiful you are getting. You're almost a man now. We shall soon have to find you a bride.'

Although he had seen no mirrors during his year in Terezin, Jan knew well enough how he must look. He had seen himself mirrored in his fellow prisoners; he knew that he resembled those other ghosts, with their grey faces and scrawny limbs. Now he saw himself reflected afresh in the admiring eyes of the Rabbi's servant-women, and in Varealina's teasing smiles. Then he glimpsed his image in the Rebbetzin's looking-glass, and the truth was confirmed. The face that looked back at him seemed older than the face he remembered, and it glowed with good health and good looks.

'So that is how I would have been if Hitler had not come to Prague,' he thought, and his eyes stung with angry tears. 'Now I know what else has been stolen from me. I would have been a handsome young man by now, instead of a scarecrow.'

Jan sat in Rabbi Loewe's study, watching as the Rabbi pored over his great books of mysticism and astronomy. A feeling of safety and contentment enveloped him like a golden haze. And yet there were questions in his mind that troubled him, and he knew that only Rabbi Loewe could provide the answers.

'Your pardon, Rabbi,' he said softly, and the old man looked up, his eyes soft and kindly in his stern face.

'Did you speak, Yankel?'

'Y-yes. I'm troubled, Rabbi. I keep thinking about Anna. She was a thief, you see, and my parents always taught me that stealing is a sin. Do you think she is in Heaven?'

Rabbi Loewe laid down his book, and smiled.

'According to all that you told me,' he replied, 'your friend stole food from those who had plenty, to give to those who were in danger of starvation. You know, don't you, that in Judaism anything is permissable in order to save life? Every sin, indeed, except murder and idolatry?'

'B-but Rabbi...'

'Now, if you were to steal food from a person who was hungry, and he starved to death as a result, then *that* would be a sin, and you would be guilty of murder. But

120

to steal from those who have plenty, in order to prevent others from starving to death, is not a sin in *my* estimation. Your Anna may have been a thief, Yankel, but I assure you she is now in Paradise. I only wish *my* place at God's right hand were as secure as hers.'

'*Your* place, Rabbi?' said Jan, surprised. 'Surely nothing can be more certain than that?'

'Oh no, Yankel, I have my own crisis of conscience. It torments me night and day. It concerns the Golem ...'

'Yossel?'

'Ah yes, I had forgotten he was your good friend. I made this man out of the clay of the river, and gave him life and humanity, and now I shall have to return him to the dank, dark river again.'

Jan felt his blood run cold.

'What, kill Yossel?' he cried. 'Oh no, surely not, Rabbi! Why?'

The Rabbi sighed.

'He has outlived his usefulness,' he said. 'Times are better now for us Jews, I am happy to say. We are no longer threatened with persecution and blood ritual accusations. But this means that the Golem has no function, other than to chop wood and sweep the kitchen, and for such menial tasks as these I do not need a Golem. His food alone costs me a fortune.'

'But, Rabbi ...'

'Besides,' the Rabbi went on, 'his great idle hands keep finding mischief to do. Every day I receive complaints about him from the townsfolk. One day he nearly burned down the bakery; another day he tossed one of our synagogue worthies into the river. He is like a mischievous child. We never know what he is going to do next. This is a risk I can no longer afford.'

'But Rabbi, he's a member of the family now.'

'I know, and we're all fond of him. Even Josefina dotes on him and feeds him with all kinds of delicacies behind my back. I've thought about it, and I've prayed, and I can find only one answer.'

Jan rubbed his eyes dolefully, and the Rabbi came forward and patted his shoulder.

'Don't be unhappy,' he said kindly. 'His death will be gentle. I'm glad you have come back, Yankel. *You* helped me create him. Now you shall help to ease his passing.'

Later that day Mordecai Markus Maisl and his wife were the Rabbi's guests at dinner. Jan had seen them at a respectful distance during his previous visit to old Prague, but had never had the opportunity of meeting them. Both were, as before, richly dressed, but Jan decided that he preferred Master Maisl to his wife. Although he looked stiff and pompous, his smile was kindly. Mistress Maisl, for *her* part, seemed much taken up with her husband's wealth and influence at Court, and also with her splendid dress, which was made of green velvet and decorated with gold lace. Jan looked at the couple, thought of the crumbling tombs in Prague's old cemetery, and marvelled.

The talk was mainly of the fine synagogue that Master Maisl was now having built to match the splendid Jewish Town Hall he had already given to the ghetto. It would be in the Renaissance style, with twenty marble columns supporting the roof, said Master Maisl. But he was having problems with his workmen; they were lazy and inefficient, and he feared they would never finish the work. Jan thought of the synagogue and the Town Hall, venerable and begrimed with age as *he* had known them, standing empty and echoing in the Jewish quarter after the Nazis had taken its inhabitants away. It was as well, he thought, that the Maisls knew him only as an orphan who occasionally visited the Rabbi's house, or he might show them visions of the future that they would prefer not to see.

'*I* would have them all whipped,' said Mistress Maisl of the workmen. 'They have no respect for you or your position.' She picked up a sugared apricot and nibbled it daintily before adding, 'Why, you have dined with the Emperor himself.'

'My dear,' said Master Maisl, smiling, 'why should these men care if I am the Emperor's friend or not? They are only concerned with earning enough to buy bread for their families, and for that I can scarcely blame them.'

'Master Maisl is a good friend to the poor,' said Rabbi Loewe to Jan, and Jan all at once remembered a story that Grandpa had told him. It seemed that Master Maisl had left a large sum of money in his will to Rabbi Loewe, to be distributed to the poor, but his wife, in her greed and stupidity, had kept the money after his death, and fate had punished her. The Emperor Rudolf had confiscated the whole of Mordecai Maisl's fortune in the name of the crown, forgetting that Master Maisl had once been his friend, and Mistress Maisl had spent her last years in poverty, dependent on the charity of others. Jan watched her as she reached for another sugared apricot, and almost felt sorry for her.

But his pity vanished when, a few moments later, Yossel the Golem came into the room, carrying a towel and a large bowl of perfumed water with which to freshen the guests' greasy hands. Mistress Maisl looked at him with distaste, and then turned to Rabbi Loewe and said, 'I see that creature is still here.'

Yossel looked at the Rabbi, puzzlement in his child-like eyes.

'Did I do something wrong, Master?' he asked.

'No, Yossel, you were very good,' replied the Rabbi gently.

After that, no one spoke again till all the guests had dipped their fingers in the bowl and Yossel had carried it back towards the kitchen. Then Mistress Maisl said, 'Rabbi, I thought you were going to get rid of that monster.'

'My dear,' interrupted Master Maisl, 'surely that is

for the Rabbi to decide?'

'Do you call him a monster?' asked Rabbi Loewe reproachfully. 'You didn't think of him as a monster when he saved us from the Jesuits and those who would brand us as ritual murderers.'

'But those times are gone,' said Mistress Maisl, 'and please God they will never come again. Besides, he is becoming impossible to control. Last week, while I was on my way to visit Mistress Grunberg, he snatched my best hat off my head and threw it in a puddle.'

Jan clapped his hands over his mouth to stifle a giggle, but the others all looked grave.

'We can't get rid of him now. He has become one of the household,' pleaded the Rebbetzin.

'But he *is* becoming a nuisance,' added Varealina sadly. 'Yesterday he took that cauldron of soup that Mother had prepared to distribute to the poor, and poured it into the river.'

The Rabbi sighed.

'I have tried to put off the evil hour,' he said, 'but I cannot postpone it any longer. It will have to be tonight. When darkness falls, I shall return him to the darkness.'

So Jan found himself walking again over the moonlit cobbles of the alley that led to the Old-New Synagogue. Once more the lantern trembled in the Rabbi's hand, as it had done on the night Yossel the Golem was created. But many things were different now. This time there were three of them, for Yossel walked between the Rabbi and Jan. And this time there was sadness rather than excitement in Jan's heart.

It seemed that Yossel guessed nothing of what was in store for him, for he chattered like a child about his plans for the coming day. He was going to help Josefina clean the kitchen, he said, and she had promised to bake him a quince pie. He wondered why she had cried when she had wished him good night.

Now the door of the synagogue loomed before them, and they climbed the steep staircase leading to the cluttered attic where the Golem had been born and where he was now going to die. Yossel had not been back to the attic since those early days, and he looked around fearfully at the shadowed room with its steep, pointed roof and its piles of musty prayer-books and tattered prayer-shawls. Jan felt for his huge hand, and pressed it reassuringly.

'Do you remember this place, Yossel?' asked the Rabbi gently.

'No,' replied Yossel.

'This is the place where I made you. Don't you remember?'

'Not very much.'

'You were created out of the clay of the river, Yossel,' said the Rabbi, 'and now it is time for you to return.'

'Why?'

'Because you are very tired. You have worked well. Wouldn't you like to rest now?'

'No. I'm *not* tired.'

Jan smiled to himself, amused by the Golem's spirit. But the Rabbi looked grave.

'You have no choice, Yossel,' he said. 'None of us has any choice. *My* turn will also come, when God wills it.'

'I don't want to go,' whimpered the Golem. 'Will it hurt?'

'No, I promise.'

'Will I ever come back?'

'Perhaps.'

Jan pressed the Golem's hand again. 'One day you *will* come back, Yossel,' he whispered, and was pleased to see the Golem smile.

'You have done well, Yossel,' repeated the Rabbi. 'You have been a good servant. Now lie down.'

Reluctantly, Yossel lay down among the prayer-shawls, his huge body resembling a fallen tree. Jan knelt beside him, still holding the giant's hand.

The Rabbi lifted the hair that concealed the Golem's brow, and Jan once again saw the metal strip engraved with the Hebrew word 'Emeth', meaning 'truth'.

'And if I take away the first letter, Yankel,' said the Rabbi, 'how will the word read then?'

'Meth,' answered Jan.

'And what does 'Meth' mean?'

Jan shivered.

'Death,' he replied.

Rabbi Loewe put forward his hand and carefully removed the first letter from the metal strip. Jan watched incredulously as the Golem's bearded face and heavily-muscled body seemed to dissolve. On the floor where he had lain there was now a huge pile of river-mud and some vast, mud-stained garments and boots. The Rabbi began to recite the Kaddish, the prayer for the dead, his voice echoing eerily under the moonlit rafters.

For some reason Jan was not thinking of Yossel the Golem any more. It seemed to him that he had just watched his mother die once again, in the hospital at Terezin.

13

The next few days were sad ones in the Rabbi's house. It seemed there was a silence and a great empty space where Yossel the Golem had been. His boots no longer thumped across the courtyard; his heavy childlike face no longer peered enquiringly round doorways, and Josefina went about with tear-filled eyes and forgot to bake any bread. Jan found himself shivering whenever he passed the Old-New Synagogue and glanced up at the triangular attic where Yossel now lay, a pile of river-mud, among the mouldering prayer-books.

Besides, he knew that he must go back to Terezin. His sisters and Grandpa were waiting for him to join them in the mysterious East. One day soon it would be his turn to go on a transport train, and they would be a family again.

He told this to the Rabbi as they sat in the study one day. Rabbi Loewe patted his shoulder, and looked grave.

'If only we could keep you safe!' he said. 'Promise, Yankel, that you'll return to us whenever you are threatened.'

'Of course I will, Rabbi. But I *must* go back. I promised my mother on her deathbed that I would look for my sisters. They must have grown quite big by now. I might not recognize them if I wait too long.'

Jan felt *almost* as brave as he sounded. These few days in the Rabbi's house had revived his courage and resolution. Besides, he had a feeling that Yossel the Golem would be waiting for him in Terezin in the person of Sergeant Kolb. But he did not tell the Rabbi this. It would be his secret, his and Yossel's.

Jan did not linger over his goodbyes. He had to go back, he explained, to his surviving family in Brno. The Rebbetzin and Varealina hugged him; Josefina wept afresh; the Rabbi pronounced a blessing over him, and he was ready for the journey. Lying in his luxurious bed that night, he clutched the golden bird and whispered, 'Take me back to Terezin!'

The familiar dizziness came upon him, and then subsided. He became aware that he was no longer lying on goose-feather pillows, but on a hard straw mattress under a scratchy blanket. In the darkness he could make out the shapes of crowded bunks. There was a pricking sensation on his back that could only be a flea.

Next morning, Jan was relieved to find that he was once again skinny and covered in sores, his stomach as cramped with hunger as if it had never known Josefina's good food. Had his absence been noticed, he wondered. Had there been a hue and cry? Somehow it had never occurred to him before that he might be missed. He plucked up the courage to ask Pavel whether he had been away, and was rewarded with an astonished look.

'*You*? Been away? Where on earth could you go?'

'I don't know,' replied Jan, trying to sound casual. 'I dreamed I got out of here, and it seemed so real that I just wondered. Are you *sure* I've been here all the time?'

'Absolutely sure. Oh, I understand, Jan. I've had that kind of dream myself.'

As the long summer days waned, and the trees turned to autumn gold, the prisoners in the camp started to prepare secretly for Rosh Hashana, the Jewish New Year, and Yom Kippur, the Day of Atonement, the two most holy religious festivals in the Jewish calendar. This was a time of prayer, repentance for past sins, and hope for the future. It was a time when God, according to Jewish tradition, judged mankind, inscribing in two great volumes the names of those who would live and those who would die in the coming year.

'And those who die here will outnumber those who live, mark my words,' said Ivo bitterly. 'It should be the Germans who are praying and fasting and repenting, not us. Every day for *us* is a Day of Atonement.'

'But won't God judge *them* too?' asked Jan.

'Not until there's more justice in this world,' Ivo replied.

Jan could only agree sadly. Back home, in the days before Hitler, these solemn High Holydays had also been a time for joy. At New Year, the family, including the grandparents, uncles, aunts and cousins, had gathered round the table in the festive candlelight to drink wine and eat apples and honey and Mother's home-made honey cake to symbolize the sweetness of the year to come. The awesome fast of the Day of Atonement had likewise been followed by feasting and light. There had been new clothes for the children, and the adults had dressed in all their finery. And after the days of repentance were over, there had been new and livelier festivals. First came the Feast of Tabernacles, when the worshippers walked in stately procession in the synagogue carrying citrons and willow branches, and the family ate its meals for a week in a specially-built hut thatched with flowers and green foliage. Last of all came the Rejoicing of the Law, a time of dancing and merriment, when the men carried scrolls of the Law encased in velvet and adorned with tinkling silver bells round the synagogue and the children followed, waving paper flags topped with lighted candles, to be rewarded with sweets for their pains.

Yes, Judaism had once offered pleasure as well as pain. Now the pleasure was all gone, and only the pain was left. And yet Jan was determined to celebrate the

Jewish New Year. Perhaps the coming year would be his last in Terezin. Perhaps Hitler would soon be defeated, and the Jews would be free to return to their old lives.

'Where are you going for the Rosh Hashana services?' asked Pavel, a few days before the festival was due.

'Do we have a choice?' said Jan in surprise. The previous year, religious services had been conducted in the children's barracks by one of their teachers, and he knew that similar arrangements were being made again.

'There are lots of services in the ghetto,' replied Pavel, 'and we can go wherever we please. Didn't you know? Just think ... there are hundreds of Rabbis among the prisoners, and each one is holding his own service.'

'*Each* one?'

'I expect so. Just imagine all those prayers rising up to Heaven from this one place, and from all those holy men! God will *have* to listen then, won't He?'

'Whose service are *you* going to?' asked Jan, not sure whether or not he should believe Pavel.

'Rabbi Leo Baeck. Have you heard of him?'

Jan admitted that he had not.

'He's a wonderful man,' said Pavel enthusiastically. 'He comes from Berlin, and he's quite old. I've heard a lot about him. He give lectures, and visits the sick, and he never gets down-hearted. The Germans once harnessed him to a garbage wagon and made him pull it through the ghetto. Do you know what he did? He discussed literature and philosophy with the man who was harnessed next to him, and he went on smiling all the while. Do you know any other Rabbi who can compare with that?'

'Rabbi Loewe,' murmured Jan without thinking.

'Who?'

'Rabbi Judah Loewe ben Bezalel.'

'But *he* lived hundreds of years ago,' replied Pavel.

'I've read about him.'

'I've read about him too,' said Jan, collecting himself quickly. 'I dreamed that I met him, that's all.'

Huddled one evening in his bunk beside Pavel, as they secretly shared Sergeant Kolb's latest sugared bun, Jan suddenly became aware of a rustling sound. He stopped chewing and listened. For a moment he seemed to glimpse a small, pointed face, rather like a weasel's, and the glimmer of a beady eye. Then it vanished, and Jan was left wondering if he had imagined it all.

'What's the matter?' whispered Pavel. 'What are you looking at?'

'I thought I saw someone watching us,' replied Jan, 'but now I'm not so sure.'

'Someone? One of the other kids?'

'That new little chap. It looked like him. I think his name's Radek.'

'Oh, *him*,' said Pavel. 'He's always watching us. I think he suspects ... you know, about the food. One of these days he's going to steal something.'

'Do you mean you *knew* all along?' cried Jan, feeling so outraged that his voice almost rose above the usual night-time whisper. 'Why didn't you warn me?'

'I didn't want to worry you.'

'Honestly, Pavel, you might have said something. Well, I'm going to watch *him* from now on.'

But keeping an eye both on Radek and on his possessions was not as easy as it sounded. The bunk had to be left unattended while Jan was at work, and Radek seemed as slippery as an eel. One day, Jan returned to his bunk to find the skinny little boy fumbling under the blanket. He looked up sharply when he saw Jan, and his pale little face convulsed with terror.

'What are you looking for?' snarled Jan, gripping the boy's scrawny arm.

'Nothing.'

131

'You must have been looking for *something*. Answer, or I'll break your arm.'

Radek began to cry.

'I thought you might have something to eat,' he moaned. 'I've seen you hiding food.'

'You're a thief,' muttered Jan. 'And thieves get hanged.'

'I'm not a thief,' sobbed Radek. 'I'm always hungry, that's all. My stomach feels like a big empty hole. Let go of my arm. You're hurting.'

Jan couldn't help feeling sorry for Radek, but forced himself to sound fierce. 'I'll let you go this time,' he said, 'but if you come anywhere near my bunk again, I'll chop you in pieces and eat you for my dinner. Understood?'

Radek nodded, gulped, and then ducked under Jan's arm and ran out of the room.

Left alone, Jan found a new fear welling up in him. Radek had been searching for food, he knew that, but might the sly little boy also have guessed at the existence of the amulet?

'It's not possible,' thought Jan. 'No one knows, not even Pavel.'

To reassure himself, he searched deep in the recesses of the mattress later that night, when all the other boys were asleep. Burrowing into the straw, his fingers closed thankfully on the golden wings and ruby eyes.

Jan sighed with relief, and slept.

The Rosh Hashana service was held in a barracks room housing about eighty people, and took place - as usual - in secret, with look-outs posted to warn of the approach of German officers. Rabbi Baeck read the prayers in low tones from a tattered prayer-book, but when he preached his sermon his voice became strong.

'We are all standing before our God,' he said, 'who judges and pardons us. While we confess our own sins, let us also refute the lies and falsehoods of those who hate us. Let us trample those lies under our feet.'

Ten days after the Jewish New Year came Yom Kippur, the Day of Atonement, when all adult Jews fasted for twenty-five hours, from sunset till an hour after sunset on the following day. It would be very different, thought Jan, from the Atonement Days of his early years. The ram's horn could not be sounded for fear of betraying the Jews to the Nazis, and there would be no feast to follow the fast, apart from the food which they had saved from their miserable rations. Jan was luckier than most of the others, for Sergeant Kolb had given him a large sugared bun which he had hidden in his bunk, to be shared with Pavel when the first stars of evening announced that the fast was over.

'You're not supposed to be fasting,' Jan told Pavel. 'You haven't had your barmitzvah yet. So I should *really* have that bun all to myself.'

'I've been fasting since I was ten,' replied Pavel proudly.

'All day?'

'Well, *nearly* all day. Anyway, in this place we fast all the time.'

'That's what Ivo said,' replied Jan. 'Don't worry, my friend, you shall have your share of my bun.'

But when the time for the shared bun drew near, Pavel was lying in his bunk, weak and ill from the effort of fasting. So Jan sat alone in an adult congregation as the last streaks of sunset faded, the sky deepened to night, and high above Heaven, Jan knew, God was finally closing and sealing His two great volumes. 'Our Father, our King,' prayed Rabbi Baeck, 'let salvation soon spring forth for us ...' The congregation then recited, 'Hear O Israel, the Lord our God, the Lord is One,' then, 'Blessed be His name whose glorious kingdom is for ever and ever,' three times and, 'The Lord, He is God,' seven times, and the Day of Atonement was over.

Jan turned to his next-door neighbour, a tall man with a white face and strangely burning eyes, and rather hesitantly wished him a happy New Year, according to custom. But the man only laughed bitterly.

'It's a long time since anyone wished me a *happy anything*,' he replied. 'Still I appreciate your good intentions. What's your name, my young friend?'

'Jan.'

'My name is Jaromil. And what are *you* hoping for this coming year, Jan?'

Jan told him how he hoped to go on a transport train to the East and find Grandpa and his sisters again, while the worshippers streamed out of the room where they had prayed all day and began to disperse towards the various barracks. When he had finished speaking, Jan became aware that Jaromil's eyes looked stranger than ever. They glowed like burning coals in the darkness.

'My young friend,' he said in a dead voice. 'Your Grandpa and your little sisters went up the chimney long ago. You must think only of saving your own life now.'

Jan stared at him, more puzzled than horrified. 'Chimney, what chimney?' he asked.

Then Jaromil began to speak, and as Jan listened he felt as if he were in some hideous dream. For Auschwitz-Birkenau, according to Jaromil, was a place of horrible death for most of the people who were sent there. Those who were strong enough to work were spared, at least to begin with. The others, the children and old and sick people, were taken straight from the transport trains to a place they were told was a bath-house. There they were ordered to undress for a shower. But the showers contained not water but a poisonous gas. When they were dead their bodies were burned in a huge crematorium whose tall chimneys belched out columns of smoke and flame by night and day.

Jan's first thought was that Jaromil must be mad. 'I don't believe you,' he gasped at last.

'I wish it were not true,' replied Jaromil sadly. 'But I had it from someone who was there. Someone who saw it all, and lived to tell the tale. Someone who escaped, disguised as an SS man, and came here to warn us. To warn us, my young friend, so that we might stage a revolution and rise up against our murderers. The trouble is that no one here believes him. *I* believe him, but no one else does.'

'I don't believe him,' Jan began, and then stopped. For he had suddenly remembered two things that had once puzzled him. There had been the postcard sent from Auschwitz-Birkenau by someone's uncle, bearing the code words in Hebrew that meant 'death' and 'gas'. And there had been the children from Bialystok, who had run away screaming 'gas' when other prisoners had tried to lead them into the delousing station. It had been whispered then that they had seen terrible things. Jan understood now what these were. It was as if the pieces of a jigsaw puzzle had suddenly fallen into place.

Jaromil reached out and gripped Jan's arm.

'For God's sake, child, don't go aboard any of those transport trains!' he cried. 'If your name comes up on the list, hide ... run away ... do anything, but don't let them take you East. Or else it will be the chimney for you too!'

Jan pulled his sleeve free from Jaromil's clutching fingers, and ran and ran. He did not stop running till he had reached the safety of his own room where those of the children who had fasted were now ravenously eating their hoarded rations.

The precious sugary bun he had looked forward to sharing with Pavel lay in its paper bag under the blanket on his bunk, but Jan had lost his appetite. He would give it all to Pavel, he thought, and then find the

135

amulet and go back to Rabbi Loewe's Prague. He would stay there for ever and ever, and never set foot in this terrible place again.

As he lay in his bunk that night, waiting for the other boys in his room to fall asleep, Jan tried not to dwell on the things the man called Jaromil had told him. The thought of Grandpa, Monika and Pavlina being gassed to death in Auschwitz-Birkenau was too dreadful to bear. He must not think of them. Jaromil had been right. He must concentrate now on saving his own life.

Earlier that evening he had given his bun to Pavel, explaining that he felt sick and could not eat it. He did not say good-bye to Pavel. He had, Jan told himself, said too many good-byes already.

Now the sound of heavy breathing told Jan that he was the last one left awake. He thrust his fingers into the slit in his mattress, fumbling for the tiny golden bird. But his fingers closed only on straw. It must have shifted, thought Jan, feeling his spine prickle with fear. It must have moved further down. His fingers felt everywhere, but there was no bird. Jan now knew that he was frightened, his palms sweating, his heart pounding. He felt everywhere, in every hole and slit in the mattress, feeling and fumbling desperately in the straw. The grey light of dawn was seeping into the room, and the other children were beginning to stir, before Jan at last accepted the awful truth.

Someone had stolen his amulet. *The golden bird had vanished.*

14

For the first time, Jan knew what real fear was. He realized that he had hitherto been protected from fear by his knowledge of the amulet hidden safe in his mattress. Now that his escape route was gone, he knew how Evald had felt, how Pavel felt, how all the other children felt. Except that the others did not know what awaited them in the East. But *he* knew.

Without the golden bird there was no way to escape. The camp was like a walled fortress, all its gates guarded day and night by armed police. If his name came up on the transport list there would be nowhere to run, no place where he could hide.

Who could the thief be? Did it matter? Even if Radek, as he suspected, had taken the amulet, Jan could not confront him; he would only deny it. Besides, he would probably have bartered it for food by now, unaware of its magical properties. The golden bird could be anywhere in the camp. It could even be taking someone else on a journey into the past. Wherever it was, the amulet was lost for ever to Jan. He would never see Rabbi Loewe, his friend and protector, again.

Then suddenly an image came into his mind. He thought of the little house on the square with the flower-filled garden, and the German sergeant who reminded him of Yossel the Golem. They were good friends, Jan told himself. Jan polished Sergeant Kolb's boots and cooked his scrambled eggs. Sergeant Kolb talked to Jan about his family and gave him bars of chocolate and sugared buns. Yes, they were good friends. If Jan's name were to appear on the transport list, Sergeant Kolb would surely protect him.

Jan did not have long to wait. Later that month another transport list was posted in the ghetto, and this time Jan's name was on it. So was Pavel Friedman's. The two boys stared at each other without speaking, and Jan found himself wondering how much Pavel suspected of the truth.

As soon as he was able to slip away, Jan ran to Sergeant Kolb's house. Dahlias and chrysanthemums were a blaze of crimson and gold in the little garden. But there was no reply to Jan's knock. Silence seemed to echo through the house. Jan knocked again, louder, feeling panic beginning to rise in him. Then the door of the adjoining house opened, and Sergeant Putsch came out. He eyed Jan with loathing, and said, 'What do you want, Jewboy? Why are you making so much noise?'

'If... if you please, sir,' stammered Jan, 'could you tell me where Sergeant Kolb is?'

'He's gone on leave for a few days. Why do you want to know?'

'I ... I ... He wanted me to clean his kitchen.'

'Well, he's said nothing to me.'

'Can you tell me when he's coming back, sir?'

'Soon. I don't know exactly. Now, go away, and stop wasting my time, or I'll break your neck.' Sergeant Putsch spat in Jan's direction, went back into his house, and slammed the door.

'He'll come back in time,' Jan told himself firmly. 'He *must* come back.'

Three days passed, but Sergeant Kolb did not reappear. Jan packed his belongings into a bag, said goodbye to those boys who were staying behind, and received some last encouraging words from Ivo. And all the time he felt as if he were made of stone. He tried not to think of the things Jaromil had told him. Surely not even Germans, thought Jan, were capable of such horrors.

Now that he was to leave Terezin, the camp suddenly seemed to him a safe and homely place. He would miss his bunk, his friends and workmates, his secret studies, and the art and music! Terezin was his life now, and ahead lay almost certain death. 'Please, Sergeant Kolb, please come back soon,' Jan prayed. 'Yossel, please come and save me!'

The last day dawned fine and sunny. All those who were being transported had been issued with numbers, which were tied with pieces of string round their necks. Those who were staying crowded around them, trying to sound cheerful as they said their good-byes. Among those was Frantisek, saved as usual from transportation by his privileged position. He hugged Jan and Pavel, and muttered something that was meant to be comforting.

'I wonder if he feels ashamed at getting special treatment,' murmured Jan to Pavel as they left their barracks for the last time and joined the prisoners who were being marched through the narrow streets towards the Hamburg Barracks.

'*Ashamed*?' retorted Pavel bitterly. 'I should think he's *glad*. Wouldn't *you* be, if you had important protectors?'

Jan did not reply. He was straining his eyes for a glimpse of Sergeant Kolb. There were Nazi guards escorting the procession, occasionally wielding a whip or truncheon or accompanied by a fierce dog pulling on its leash, but no sign of the clumsy, benevolent officer who reminded him of Yossel the Golem. Jan's knees trembled and he could scarcely walk. He heard the endless thud of boots on the cobbles, and was aware of faces peering from the ghetto windows, bidding them a wordless good-bye.

The courtyard of the Hamburg Barracks was already crowded when Jan and Pavel arrived. There seemed to be thousands of prisoners crammed together in the yard, mostly old people and children, but more kept arriving and adding to the congestion, clutching their bags and shabby suitcases and anxiously looking around for friendly faces. Some of the smaller children cried and were consoled by adults. Jan saw Friedl Dicker-Brandejsova trying to look calm while three of the little girls who had drawn the 'happy' pictures clutched nervously at her skirt. He heard the one called Julie whimper, 'I'm thirsty, will they give us something to drink when we get there?' and Friedl reply, 'I'm sure they will, darling,' in a voice that was meant to be reassuring.

'So much for art, and artists,' thought Jan. 'What did it matter if the pictures we drew were happy or sad? It's all come to the same thing in the end.'

Above the hum of the prisoners' voices he could hear all kinds of other sounds - the barking of dogs, the shouted commands of SS guards, and the lilting tones of an orchestra playing a polka from *The Bartered Bride*. The last time he had been here, recalled Jan, it had been to see Evald off on the same journey. Now it was *his* turn to have his name checked against the transport list and then to pass through the massive gates leading from the courtyard to the railway station, where the transport train waited.

Seen in close-up, the train came as a shock. Jan had been expecting a normal passenger train, like the ones with comfortable leather seats that had taken him and his family on holiday in the happy pre-war days. *This* train, its engine belching heavy smoke, was no more than a linked chain of trucks without seats or windows, of the type farmers used to take cattle to market. Batches of prisoners were being crammed into these trucks so tightly that Jan wondered, with a thrill of fear, how they would be able to move or stand or even breathe. Yet the guards continued to pack them in. Worst of all, the Commandant, whom the children had called 'uncle' during the Red Cross visit, was now rushing up and down the platform brandishing a walking-stick with which he thrashed those poor prisoners who did not move quickly enough for his liking. 'It's true,' thought Jan as the pressure of the crowd carried him towards the train. 'Everything that Jaromil told me is true.'

Suddenly his heart leaped with joy. A few yards ahead, directly in front of him, Sergeant Kolb was standing. 'He's come back in time to save me,' thought Jan exultantly. And without thinking what he was doing or saying, he ran towards the Sergeant, shouting 'Yossel!'

But there was no reply. Sergeant Kolb's eyes were looking through him without recognition. Then something happened that made Jan's blood freeze. He saw Sergeant Kolb lunge forward and viciously kick an old woman who had tripped while trying to get into one of the trucks. Watching in horror, Jan wondered how he could ever have likened the Sergeant to Yossel. His face was brutish and incomprehending, with none of the Golem's childlike wonder.

Then suddenly Jan understood. While Rabbi Loewe had created his Golem as a power for good, to watch over the ghetto, Hitler had created *his* Golems, his own robots as a force for evil.

As he stood trembling, Jan felt himself being propelled forward. One of the crowded trucks loomed before him. He saw ranks of faces rising above other faces. 'There's no room here!' he wanted to cry. But before he could utter a sound, he was pushed into the tangle of white faces. The door closed behind him, and he heard a rasping sound as the bolts were drawn and the padlocks fastened.

Then the train moved on, carrying Jan, Pavel, Friedl

and all the others to their dreadful destination.

As Sergeant Hans Kolb and his friend and neighbour walked home together after the train had gone, Sergeant Putsch asked, 'Why did that boy call you Yossel?'

'I didn't hear that,' replied Sergeant Kolb, who was thinking about his evening meal.

'Yes, he did,' persisted Sergeant Putsch. 'That's a Jew name. Are you a Jew?'

Sergeant Kolb stopped and stared at his friend in dismay.

'Me a Jew?' he said. 'Don't say such things, not even in fun. Do I look like a Yossel?'

'You liked the kid, didn't you?' Sergeant Putsch went on.

'He was all right. He made good scrambled eggs. I'll have to find somebody else now.'

'Don't worry. They're two a penny.'

They walked on, and soon reached the cottages in whose gardens autumn flowers were still a blaze of colour. Then, laughing and joking, they went in to supper.